A Healer's Tale London

King Atlas V

Atlantean V Bookworks
Naples, FL

King Atlas V/Atlantean V Bookworks
P.O. Box 9651
Naples, FL/34101
https://www.amazon.com/author/kingatlasv

Publisher's Note: This is a work of fiction. Names, characters, places, and incidents are a product of the author's imagination. Locales and public names are sometimes used for atmospheric purposes. Any resemblance to actual people, living or dead, or to businesses, companies, events, institutions, or locales is completely coincidental.

Book Layout & Design ©2017 - BookDesignTemplates.com

Image E-Book Cover: Copyright: <a href='https://www.123rf.com/profile_gjee'>gjee / 123RF Stock Photo</a>

A Healer's Tale London/ King Atlas V -- 1st ed.
ISBN Ebook 978-0-9985856-2-8; ISBN Paperback 978-0-9985856-3-5

Dedicated to St. James

Long Live the King

–Unknown

Table of Contents

1.

T HE THAMES RIVER was unusually calm and blue this, a Saturday, in the fall of 2017. The Thames Clippers were zipping down the river. It was 3:00 P.M. BST, on a Saturday afternoon. The sixty-two-year old father from Westminster, Connecticut, was trailing at least five steps behind his fleet footed daughter, a resident of the Borough of Southwark, of thirty years of age, and his youthful wife of sixty years, as they paced down the crowded Riverwalk on the south embankment of the Thames. Their blonde pony tails tossed back and forth, as their matching Nike sneakers with bright green swooshes pounded on the pavement.

The father enjoyed the radiant sun, as it seemed to calm down the arthritic pain in his knees from so much walking. They were returning from a long walk from Southwark Bridge on the north side of the Thames River, down to the Westminster Abbey, and back, mostly along the Riverwalk on the north embankment. They had returned to the south of the Thames River over the London Millennium Foot-bridge that linked the City of London, the square mile of city within a city, back to the Borough of Southwark. Winston turned back to admire the dome of St. Paul's Cathedral as they reached the southern embankment. Up ahead was the Playhouse, where they had evening tickets for Romeo and Juliet on Sunday night. Further south was the modern museum, Tate Modern, a visit for the next day, certainly planned.

They continued east up the southern Riverwalk, firmly in the Borough of Southwark. A stroll through the Borough Market was next for some British pastries, for an afternoon snack.

The father, with combed over hair that was light brown with the aid of his hair assistant, was in khaki slacks and boat shoes, that pinched his feet after 20,000 steps of walking. His name was Winston. He had marveled at the statues of Winston Churchill throughout the city, particularly, in front of Parliament.

They walked underneath the London Bridge, followed by a circuitous path to Tower Bridge. Across the way was the Tower of London. They had spent the day at the Tower of London on Friday, the first day of their visit.

His wife of thirty-five year's marriage, Mary, and his daughter, Elizabeth, were flummoxed by his slow pace.

"Hurry up Dad!" Elizabeth belted out. "We would like to grab a dinner at a pub before we go home!"

Winston admonished their warning, and caught up to them. Certainly, a new pair of walking sneakers were in order for the balance of the trip. They stopped just before Tower Bridge.

The two women stopped and went into a boutique gift shop. Winston took the opportunity to rest on a bench, that had just been vacated, by one of the few old couples he had seen the entire day.

As he rested, he saw a strange looking cloud float over the horizon above the Tower of London. It seemed to be shaped like a continent-one that he did not recognize. It dispersed. A second cloud rolled by. It appeared to be a Castle of sorts, or large Temple. Finally, a third cloud rolled by. Of course, it looked like something. Some sort of Palace.

Winston felt shaken somewhat, and felt adrenaline surging through his body. It felt like he had been hit by a slow lightning bolt, that just kept striking, but not with enough power to endanger him.

Frightfully, he stood, and looked around. All appeared normal. There were no thunder clouds in the sky. No Lightning bolts anywhere. His wife and daughter returned, somewhat frustrated that they had to endure his anticipated slow pace again. This time, Winston lead the way. Mary and Elizabeth hurried to keep pace now, looking at each other cockeyed at the sudden energetic exhibition by the hobbled "old man".

Winston looked at all the pedestrians and passersby. Something was different, way different. It appeared he could see an aura around them. It appeared he could see the ones who were happy and joyful, and the ones who were suffering from some malady, or distraught. A man, severely hunched, across in a small park, just pass London Bridge on their way back, and squatting behind a park bench, appeared to watch him with hawk like eyes. He stared back, not in defiance, but with empathy. The man with the hunch in his back, seemed to show a glimmer of a smile, even with his crooked brown teeth, barely discernible in the shade of a giant oak tree.

Winston sensed energy flowing through his body. His knees seem to flex like the limbs of a willow tree. His growling stomach seemed to no longer concern itself with acid indigestion, and its normal recalcitrant ways. Most surprisingly, he saw a glimpse of himself in a bicycle mirror.

"Not a chance, that can't be me," he mumbled.

And they walked to the pub for dinner.

2.

THE BURGER WAS DRIPPING JUICES that soaked the bun. No cheese adorned the beef. He took his first bite, much to his delight. Elizabeth was startled at how consumed he was by such a simple act. Mary tossed her salad around with her fork, looking for her first dainty bite. Her pinky flared out in a typical gesticulation, as she found her first morsel, an olive, for tasting. Elizabeth watched both her parents, and joined the task at hand. She only ordered a cup of soup. Her appetite was typically scant.

"So, Mum, what do you think of London?" Elizabeth asked to break the verbal silence. She huffed somewhat, as if the question was forced.

"Quite extraordinary. It is so plush, so green. I have never seen so many trees and flowers in a city before. It is quite breathtaking and relaxing," her Mum spoke first, eyeing Winston for his manners and way of eating.

"I believe greatness was ever present in London throughout its remarkable history. The blend of the historical sites and modern buildings is awe-inspiring and breathtaking. The mixture of royalty and modern politics is marvelous. The people are friendly and smart. I love the accent. But to them, I have such an American accent!" Her father added.

Elizabeth had expected such stock answers from her parents, neither of whom had traveled much from Connecticut. But her father seemed off. Something was different. His appetite seemed ravenous. Unusually, so, she thought. She watched him more adeptly. Mary seemed to notice her daughter's new found attention to her father bothersome.

"Shall we go to London's most famous department store tomorrow?"

Elizabeth turned to her mother. "Sure, why not. Dad can take a walk in Hyde Park while we shop!"

Winston looked up, his burger fully devoured.

"That was simply the best burger I have had, ever! Love these London pubs! And now to wash it down with a nice London pub draft beer!"

"And?"

"Yes, we shall walk to the department store tomorrow. I will be glad to explore the park, and the monument of Prince Albert."

Winston suddenly harked back to his epiphany on the Thames. *What was that I saw in the skies? What was that energy jolt! Why did all the people look so strange, so lit up? What is going on?*

He looked up, again. Mary and Elizabeth were talking about fashion, the Princess Di collection at Kensington Palace that they would see tomorrow as well. He saw the same light above them.

Is it their aura? How could that be? Is it their soul, the light or shadow of their souls? Mary has some dark spots. What are they?

His mind seemed to spiral outwardly. He thought he was experiencing an out of body experience, during the day, not in a dream. He watched himself and his wife and daughter.

He was talking again. About NFL football in London. About the New England Patriots, and Brady's and Belichick's quest for a sixth Super Bowl. He liked hearing that discussion. But he seemed to roam away. Away from the small pub next to the Borough's Market. Across the way was the man with the hunch in his back. The man looked up, as if to see him. But he did not. *He may sense my presence. What is going on?* He continued to drift. He saw two young British males in their late twenties, sitting in their wheel chairs, gazing at the river, lost in conversation. They, too, seemed to stop their conversations midstream, as if to say hello to him. They each looked around, saw nothing, and continued their talking. They talked of their morbid lives, without work, relying on the public dole, and the mercy of passersby. One was without legs, the other was with stumps only. He had prosthetics at home, but seldom used them. A young woman about thirty walked by them. She wore a scarf to cover her face. Her face was defaced with terrible burns. The two males found her attractive to watch- one of their few remaining enjoyable moments, watching a pretty girl walk by, until they saw her face, mocked her and looked away. She saw their scorn and dissatisfaction. She pulled her scarf a little tighter. And marched on. She thought she recognized one of the men. But she wasn't sure. Maybe someone from her wild past.

A small boy was on a bench nearby. He saw the rebuff and felt badly. He himself had lost all of his hair from his chemo treatment.

"I think you are pretty," he said.

The young woman turned to look at him. Stunned, she walked over to him, and gave him a kiss on the cheek, and then gave him a small daisy.

He grabbed it and held it tightly. But he walked a few steps to the railing by the river.

"Here, Mister, this is for you, from a pretty girl, who gave it to me. It smells very fresh."

The blind man grabbed the small flower and sniffed it. He smiled, and patted the boy on his shoulder. His senses were heightened by his lack of sight.

"May you be well, young lad."

The boy, the young woman, and the blind man, suddenly paused and looked around.

"Do they see me, sense me?" Winston asked.

"What do you mean by that!" Mary barked out.

Winston snapped back to the pub. He appeared startled at the question. He looked sheepishly at Mary, but said nothing.

Elizabeth was more convinced now, that something was indeed strange about her father.

"Dad, are you all right? You are acting quite strangely since we left the Riverwalk. The way you ate your burger. Senseless babbling. I don't know."

"I am fine. Just a bit off, I suppose. Jet lag is surely to blame. A pub pie may solve all of the issues!"

"And a good night's sleep, too, Dad!"

"Indeed."

Elizabeth exhaled, and then looked at her nails. She flipped her ponytail, as a young man walked by, wearing a rugby shirt of his favorite team. Mary noticed, but pursed her lips in indifference. Mary grimaced slightly in pain. A pain she had felt before in her chest. It was a tighter pain this time. Elizabeth noticed the flinch, and looked inquisitively at her mother.

No comments were made.

The three of them finished their drinks. It was still light out, but barely. They headed home to the flat rented by Elizabeth on Southwark Bridge Lane.

3.

MARY HAD CRASHED immediately upon returning to the flat. Elizabeth had retired shortly thereafter to her room, where she shared her large bed with her mother. She took the heavy brace off her knee, injured when she played college sports in America. She stretched her aching back, sore from her scoliosis.

Winston was relegated to the couch in the first floor living area. But the keys to the flat lay on the table next to the couch.

He stared at the keys. Suddenly, they appeared to drift into the air. He thought he was hallucinating. Then the keys seemed to do a dance, marching to the chimes of the clock, that had just chimed at eleven o'clock. They beckoned him. He shook. He grabbed a blanket and pulled it over him. But he still shook. He closed his eyes, partly in fear, and partly in denial. But his ears picked up the jingle. The chimes stopped. He peaked out. The keys were silent and not moving.

I must have been dozing. Half dream state. I like that state. It is fun to watch the bizarre movies our minds play for us. But just an amalgamation of images and sounds our brain assimilated over the days prior. But where did I see keys jingle to life. AH, Elizabeth likes to play with her keys, wrapping them repeatedly around her fingers. A small obsessive behavior, one not worthy of concern.

Winston grabbed his smart phone. He checked out the college football scores. The afternoon games were over. His Nebraska team had won. The Red Sox would not play until 1:00 A.M. He read some news feeds.

He thought about the upcoming NBA season. The Warriors and Cavs had taken the last three titles. Could the Celtics make a run at their eighteenth title? They were dynamic and deep. Just maybe.

He forgot the keys. He closed his eyes. Again, he appeared to disengage from his body. Soon he was hovering over a park. Underneath the bench, was a dirty old blanket. He saw a large bump protruding from the blanket. He saw the face of the man with a hunch in his back. The man stirred, and peaked out from his blanket. Winston looked deeply into his eyes.

I see his spirit!

"Save me!"

The man with a hunch in his back, returned the cover of his dirty blanket over his face. Winston was shocked.

Did he just speak to me?

Winston drifted away, almost aimlessly, as if blown by the gentle autumn nighttime breeze. Soon he was looking into a window of a flat in the Borough of Southwark, not far from his flat.

A curtain was slightly pulled back. A small boy peered out. A tear ran down his face. A sparkle of light lit up his iris on his right eye. Winston looked deep into his eyes. The boy nodded, and rubbed his eyes, and closed the curtain.

Winston drifted further away to the south. Soon he was at a soldier's home. The two young men he had seen earlier were still up, playing gin rummy. They stopped and put their cards down. And said nothing.

"Maybe someday," the soldier blurted.

"Hey, not a chance, no such thing as fairy tales!" the football player responded.

"Someday," the football then said hopefully.

Only one was a soldier. The other was his friend, and once one of the premier football players in the Premier League. He had suffered terribly, in a horrific accident, all caused by his inebriation and wild lifestyle. His regret was as painful as his loss of his two legs. But the older women he had slammed into with his luxury automobile, had fully recovered, as well as her granddaughter. Now, he suffered alone, penniless from the lawsuits and resident care bills, and forgotten by the masses of adoring football fanatics.

Winston felt himself float again, all the way to Mayfair. There was a fabulous row of beautiful homes. He passed Hyde Park on the way, feeling an energy below him. But soon he was hovering in the basement inside one of the most expensive homes. There was the young woman he had seen hours ago in another out of body sojourn, with the terrible scars on her face. He saw flames and a burning home. A small dog had perished. He saw a tear drop from her eye, as she was looking at a picture of her little dog. He watched as she felt her scars on her face, looked at a small mirror, as if hoping they would disappear, and then dropped her face into her awaiting hands.

He watched and fully sensed her emotions and thoughts, almost as if he became one with her. She sobbed for freedom from the bondage of her face. She felt hideous, but knew her soul was beautiful. And she had been the prettiest of girls, until that fateful day when she was nineteen. If she had not tried to save her dog, her face would still be so fair. But she had saved the priceless painting in her study. There it stood, a portrait of a Princess, from faraway times, a faraway artist, of historic repute. All of her parent's wealthy friends and doctors, though, could not put her face back together again. Each plastic surgery, just made it worse. She had put a stop to the nonsense, and just buried herself in her own world, locked in her parent's fine home, with the secretive walks along her favorite river, her lone escape, and, of course, her foray into paintings, down deep into the cavernous basement of her parent's home. *Someday, maybe my paintings will be pretty and priceless, too.*

Winston returned, or he felt as if he returned, as his body had never left, to the couch. He trembled in uncertainty over the newfound translucence of his being. He questioned his mind, but fell into a slumber, but not so deep, because his dream state took over.

Soon his mind was flying, flying deep into his past, the most ancient of pasts. His was his dream state, for certain, but it was so real.

There he was. At least ten feet tall. Bronzed, and athletic. He was young, but wore a crown. He was at a large Palace, just like the one he saw in the clouds. It was immense, and reminded him of ancient Roman architecture, and maybe it was the prehistoric architecture that had carried over to the Greeks and Romans. He was on the steps. Across the way, a saw what appeared to be a magnificent Temple, replete with enormous columns, and adorned with ornate sculptures.

It was a gorgeous day. The skies were bright blue. He looked across a bay. There was a small land barrier that formed the bay, a safe harbor from the ocean. In the ocean, he saw twelve monumental rock pillars protruding from the ocean and protecting the city, all formed by natural rock formations. White puffy clouds floated above the monuments in the sky.

But then everything changed. The skies suddenly churned with dark clouds, and blue and red lightning bolts crashed into the city around him. He could see across the land mass barrier. Gigantic waves pounded to shore and against the monumental rock pillars. The protective pillars crashed to the sea. Minor tremors shook the ground beneath him. His citizens were leaving in droves, testing the nasty seascape. As he looked around, not many were left.

He walked to the other side of the Palace. Out in the distance, he saw an impressive mountain range. Lava flows were relentlessly marching toward the city.

Slowly, he had memories, of his youth, in this most ancient of places. He was once an Olympic sprint champion. He saw his most beautiful wife, now his Queen, and one with the purest of beings. He recalled now what was his continent. It was the same shape as the cloud he had seen that day on the river. The continent was perishing. He had been a healer, with special powers from beyond, or maybe from within. But he had not saved the continent. His scientists had informed him the axis of the earth was actually tilting. The doomsday was upon them.

Winston awoke from his dream. It was so vivid. It was so real. He was actually there, he certainly believed now. *ATLANTIS*. He bolted upright.

Light shimmered off the keys. He grabbed them, put on a light jacket and long pants, and his Nike walking shoes. He tore out the door. The air was cool, and refreshing. A fog had set in, not enough to block his sight, but enough where he felt the water droplets. He wasn't sure where he was heading, but he just walked towards the river. It was almost midnight.

As he walked up the Riverwalk on the south of the Thames, there were few passersby. One asked him for money. He was not a thief. Winston gave him five pounds.

Soon he saw a small park like area near London Bridge. He slowly approached. There was a bench. Underneath the bench, he saw a dirty blanket with a lump underneath. Flashbacks overwhelmed him. *Certainly, this must still be a dream.*

But the dream turned real. The man with the hunch back, foul of drunken breath, and red of eye, peeked above his blanket again.

"I knew you would come back! Save me if you can!"

The man with the hunch back climbed out of his makeshift home. He tossed the blanket aside. He bowed before Winston.

"I know you are a King! I have seen you in my dreams for years. And a Supreme Healer. I ask for your mercy and for my health and well-being."

The man with the hunch back knelt before Winston. Winston took his hands and lifted him up from the bench.

"I am the once and former King of Atlantis. Upon my word, you shall be healed. So, it shall be said, so, it shall be done. You are hereby healed. Go, and serve the common good."

Winston and the man locked eyes, as if there were a familiarity beyond the last twenty-four hours. Winston let go of his hands, and walked away.

The man with the back with no hunch, stood straight as a soldier. His breath was clear, his strength returned. He felt ebullient.

"Long Live the King!" He belted out with a ferocity that reverberated across the river. The few passersby turned their heads, but kept going.

Winston walked back to the west on the southern River-walk. A woman in her fifties approached him, starring at the moonlight reflection on the river that followed her on her walk. It was her path to heaven, for sure, she knew in her heart. He saw her aura and glow. She was dying of cancer. She had left her hospice, to enjoy her river just one more time.

The woman turned as Winston was about to pass her. Their eyes met simultaneously. She felt a magnetic pull towards him. He held her hands.

"I am the once and former King of Atlantis. Upon my word, you shall be healed. So, it shall be said, so, it shall be done. You are hereby healed. Go, and serve the common good."

The woman felt enlivened and enlightened. She knew she was cured and fully healed. She felt twenty years younger. She cried softly to herself, and recalled the chant she had heard moments earlier.

"Long Live the King!" she belted out. She glanced back to look at the moonlight on the river. A cloud had passed over the moon: the moonlight was gone. *No heaven in my immediate future! Mummy, I will see you a bit later, indeed! And of course, I shall make my list tomorrow to serve the common good.*

Winston continued his stroll, walking at a slow pace. He was startled as he approached the railing of the Riverwalk. There was the blind man he had seen in his dreams. He was still standing in the same spot. He put his hands on the blind man's shoulder. He saw tears streaming from his eyes, as his dark glasses were removed, revealing two glass eyes.

"I felt you earlier. I knew you would come. I have not had my sight since I was twenty-one, when I lost both eyes on a fall off of a mountain trail. God Bless You!"

Winston, not sure of what to do, as his normal self, but his new found former incarnated spirit from Atlantis, rattled inside him. His energy was still at the highest level. He was still emblazoned with energy from somewhere, he knew. He held the hands of the blind man.

"I am the once and former King of Atlantis. Upon my word, you shall be healed. So, it shall be said, so, it shall be done. You are hereby healed. Go, and serve the common good."

The man, saw a bright light first. He knew it was energy from the man, the King, before him. He saw the face of Winston, and bowed. He then roared as he turned and saw the river. The moonlight was there. It was his new path through life. He was overcome with emotion and joy. He hugged Winston, and headed to Chelsea. He would surprise his Mum in the morning. Thoughts of a lost love surfaced. Soon, he would work with and for vision-both literally and figuratively. He could not wait.

"Long Live the King!" he rejoiced.

Three more times on his walk back home, the chants were repeated. An elder man stricken with horrific arthritis, a young girl, who had lost her hand in a boating accident, and an escaped patient from the local mental health hospital. Six exuberant and joyful souls looked through the lens of what might be their future new lives.

Winston walked up to the bedroom where his wife and daughter were fast asleep, and snoring. He held each of their right hands against his heart.

"I am the once and former King of Atlantis. Upon my word, you shall be healed. So, it shall be said, so, it shall be done. You are hereby healed. Go, and serve the common good," he softly whispered.

They stirred, but remained in their deep slumber. He laughed softly under his breath. "Long Live the King! Long Live the King!" He thought that maybe the homage was needed to cement the healing process. *Just in case.*

4.

WINSTON AWOKE at sunrise. He saw the keys. He knew his two gals would need another two hours, at least, of resting sleep. *They are not moving. But they want me to take them and leave for the morning. But wait, I did go out last night. No, that was a dream. But I recall going to the park by the river. There was the man with the hunchback. I said something to him. He appeared joyous. There were five others.*

He walked to Boroughs Market and bought a most delicious almond croissant. People were carrying on normally. No chatter about a King, or Supreme Healer. He saw the London Newspaper headlines. Nothing of note. Brexit was foremost in the narrative, as lawmakers ramped up after the summer vacation period. A new viral inhibitor had passed beta testing with flying colors. The battle of humankind versus the microbe world was ferocious, but leading scientific researchers were hounding their foes with new technologies and discoveries.

Winston drew in a large breath, and headed for the river. He jaunted off toward the Tower Bridge. He purchased a large iced tea with blackberries along the way. It was so refreshing.

But as he walked back from the Tower Bridge, the din of voices became audible at an individual level. He seemed to hear every conversation. His mind assembled massive bits of information and data. It was if his mind was some sort of supercomputer. He saw the auras of his passersby. He saw happiness and sadness. He knew who was not healthy, and who was giddy. Most were stable and content. A troubled youth walked by him. He simple touched him. He did not speak. The kid's aura changed before him. The kid smiled. Winston saw a dark cloud of smoke like air leave the lad's body.

"So, the King is real after all, Long Live the King!" the lad thought in his mind, while gazing at Winston. Only Winston could hear his thoughts.

Winston kept to his march home. Underneath London Bridge, he thought, for sure, he could hear the cries of the ancient past, where much torture had occurred in the torture chambers. But he could not help those souls of long ago.

But I cannot help anyone now either. That is simply impossible. My dream world is overtaking me! Or is it?

As he passed London Bridge, and saw daylight again, he saw the small park. He saw the bench, too. The blanket was gone.

Surely, a dream.

But then he saw the trash can. Hanging slightly over the edges was a ragged old blanket. It was the blanket. Winston searched around with his eyes. He did not see anyone with a hunch back. But why would he, the hunch back was gone. He did not see anyone that resembled the man with the former hunch back. He pounded his Nike shoes on down the Riverwalk. He looked at the steeple of St. Paul's. *Maybe I should head to the cathedral and pray.*

Winston stopped dead in his tracks. On a bench overlooking the river, on this bright day with brilliant, cloudless blue skies, he saw three people. He saw their auras. He heard their conversations. The young woman with the scarf, the boy who called her pretty, and the man holding a daisy. He heard his words, that he dreamt of saying repeatedly the night before.

They are real people. He can see. He is watching the people. That older woman, standing next to the bench. She is not well. She resembles him. She must be his mother, his mum. The girl has taken off her scarf. She is not paying heed to the passersby who are squeamish at her looks. She ignores their rude comments. She is otherwise so fair, and so athletic in her physique. Her hair, her thick flowing long auburn hair shines so brightly in the suns' rays. And the boy is dying- maybe, any day. The chemo failed. He is certainly in pain. He left his hospice. All this I see now. Where are his parents. AH, he is an orphan. But he is happy. He is smiling. Will they recognize me? Am I real? Is the King of Atlantis me, or another soul using my body as a medium? No, it is me, both then and now. I must help them, and others, but keep under the radar.

The man who was once blind, felt his presence before he saw him. Winston knew. He heard his thoughts. *The King is here. Long Live the King.*

The man held his arm across the young woman and boy. They became silent. There was a sudden parting of the swarm of passersby. A gap in the long flow of people meandering the Riverwalk this Sunday morning. Maybe they had gone to a cathedral, or a breakfast place. But there was an opening. Winston approached. There was silence. He did not hear the cacophony of voices and thoughts. He saw the light from his own soul radiating in the eyes of his three beholders of his form. They knew his presence. He grabbed the young woman's hands first. She smiled, and threw back her hair with a delightful thrust. She gazed deeply into his eyes. It was as if she could see Atlantis herself. The young boy held her tightly. The former blind man grabbed the arm of the bench tightly in anticipation of the miracle upon them. His balding head glistened in the sun, as his square jaw clenched tightly. His mother gasped. She sat down on the grass nearby in exhaustion from the mere seconds that had passed.

"I am the once and former King of Atlantis. Upon my word, you shall be healed. So, it shall be said, so, it shall be done. You are hereby healed. Go, and serve the common good."

The young woman could only smile. There were no mirrors. She shouted out, "Long Live the King!" She stood and kissed Winston on the cheek. He saw her wondrous beauty, seemingly more than before the fire.

"Use your paintings," was all Winston could muster to say to her. He then took the hands of the small boy.

"I am the once and former King of Atlantis. Upon my word, you shall be healed. So, it shall be said, so, it shall be done. You are hereby healed. Go, and serve the common good."

Winston saw the aura of the boy turn to white. All the gray from the cancer was gone. His hair was frothy and black on the top of his skull. The boy pushed back his hair, as if he were Tarzan. He then belted out a call to the wild, like Tarzan, his hero in his dream world, followed by the now mandatory "Long Live the King!" He kissed the young woman on the cheek, and held her tightly.

"I would love to have a little brother, you know," she said as tears flowed freely from her bedazzling blue eyes, bluer than ever from the picture-perfect sky.

"I would love that so much," he blurted out.

The young woman, now spectacularly prettier than anyone Winston, the young boy and the former blind man had ever seen, arose to leave.

"Thank you so much for bringing the King to us, John Masterson. I am so dearly happy that you have found your sight. And that girl that you once left in your state of self-pity and despondence. You should go see her. GO now!" The young woman said in joy.

"I shall, and thank you, for always bringing me your home baked cookies all of these years, Amanda Worthington. You are the kindest of souls. You are indeed a lovely Princess once again. A true beauty! No longer the Beast!"

"But Your Grace, there is one more healing, is there not?" the young boy, Mark Buckingham, bravely asked the King.

Winston walked to the older woman sitting on the grass. He saw that she was dying from complications from diabetes. He grabbed her hands. The other three held each other's hands in unison. They braced again for another miracle. At least that is how they saw it.

"I am the once and former King of Atlantis. Upon my word, you shall be healed. So, it shall be said, so, it shall be done. You are hereby healed. Go, and serve the common good."

The older woman felt wonderful. But she softly spoke before her eyes peacefully shut for a morning nap.

"Long Live the King!"

The parted sea of people closed. Winston departed, waving good-bye, and smiling with his perfectly straight white teeth. He seemed unconcerned over the cacophony of voices overwhelming him again. In the distance, he could hear the voices of the two he loved so dearly, along with his daughter Anne back in Boston. They were arising for the day. Deciphering the hundreds of voices, subconsciously of course, he surmised that musings of his healings had not spread. A discreetness had seemed to grip his healed friends, as he called them.

"Mum, it is quite odd, but both my knee and my back feel great this morning, maybe better than ever, so odd," Elizabeth sheepishly said, brushing her platinum blonde hair away from her blue eyes, still dark from the prior evening's make up.

Mary only eyed her. Her chest pain was gone, too. Her congestive heart failure had dogged her for years. She felt very alive and energetic.

"What is going on, my dear!"

"What do you mean? Where is Dad?"

"I don't know. Let's text him."

Winston saw the text.

"On my way home. Just had a delightful walk along the river. See you soon. I shall bring back some Americano coffee! Love you both!"

5.

WINSTON ARRIVED at the flat within fifteen minutes. He opened the door to see two very cheery eyed women. Mary hugged him with a passionate embrace. Elizabeth followed suit. They seemed to have been crying.

"Why the gleeful look?"

Neither would respond. He just stared at them. He knew. He just didn't know if they knew it was him.

"Shall we go to the Tate modern museum?" Winston asked, his eyes seemingly sparkling to his family members.

"Of course, we shall enjoy some fine culture today," Mary confirmed, eyeing her husband ever so questioningly and suspiciously.

Winston just stared at her. He did not where or how to begin. And his wife had always openly and vigorously challenged him on his discussions of the paranormal, parallel universes, wormholes, other dimensions and of course, the existence of Atlantis, other than as an island sunk off of Crete by a tsunami.

"I am ready and refreshed from my morning walk along the river. Quite invigorating, I have much more energy today. Boundless, I do say! Winston beamed," thrusting his shoulders back.

"Cheerio!" Elizabeth giggled. She knew of her father's interest in the unknown, but did not link him to her suddenly revived back and knee.

"The dry air is miraculous for my joints," she continued.

"Oh, for sure," Mary acknowledged, to appease herself. And the fresh, highly oxygenated air was certainly the reason she felt so lively, so it seemed, in any event.

The three left the flat and darted down the road to the museum. They were soon marveling at modern paintings, and soaking in the arts. The museum was full with mostly Londoners, but there was a tour of Aussies that were quite jovial and boisterous. Winston joined their tour, to learn what he could from the tour guide. He learned from the idle conversations of the touring Aussies as well.

In the back, was a young man. He was without his right arm. He seemed distant, and paid little heed to the tour guide or the modern art.

Winston overheard some women talking about Peter. That must be his name. Poor Peter had lost his right arm in a shark attack in Australia, off of Sydney, while surfing late in the evening, the year before. He had been inwardly focused ever since, his bombastic personality quite stunted.

Winston eventually left the group to look for his wife and daughter. They were no longer in the café, likely having sauntered back again to other parts of the museum. It was then he saw the two men he had seen in his night vision, the night before, playing gin rummy, and the day before in their wheel chairs by the Thames River.

The soldier looked expectantly at Winston. His mind's eye recalled the two appearances by Winston, once at the river, and once at the soldier's home. Winston surveyed the situation, and determined the group was incognito to the museum goers, not on anyone's radar. The former athlete lowered his head in shame and with humbleness. Winston felt their sorrow and loneliness. Winston addressed them with a kind and caring attitude.

"Today is 'someday'. I shall heal you. I ask only that you not create a commotion. I will try once more to heal you, who I expect are my former citizens of Atlantis. Or so it seems that must be the case, but I am not sure. Stay in your chairs until you leave the museum."

"Someday did come!" They both exclaimed.

Oddly, so it seemed to Winston, Peter, from Australia had ventured to the café. He seemed drawn to Winston.

"I saw you walking with us earlier. I felt some type of energy when I was near you. Even a tingling in my shoulder. I am here, if there is anything to this matter. I see some soldiers are here. Maybe they felt the energy as well," Peter Taylor spoke in a hurried and excited voice, for the first time in months. His broad shoulders and narrow hips, and short cropped blonde hair certainly fit his appearance as a surfer. His accent gave his country of origin away.

The former athlete looked upon Peter Taylor.

"I am suspecting a former surfer from Down Under? I see a shark worked on you a bloody bit. I am so sorry to see that! I am John Chester Jones. I am not a soldier, but James Tudor here was, and he lost some limbs for the freedom of his country. He and I were childhood friends from Birmingham. He always wanted to be a soldier. I was an athlete. I played football, but my career was ended in a car accident, one that was indeed my fault, and one that I regret every day, more than the end of my career," Jones admitted his miseries, while brushing back his jet-black hair exposing his rather low hairline, and bushy black eyebrows, that made him look like a Roman emperor.

James Tudor had shaved his head, but nonetheless smoothed his stubbles, as if on cue from his friend. Peter was amused at the simultaneity of the brush back, and smooth back.

Peter thought of his family in Sydney, who he had left in the depths of his despair. James thought of his divorced wife, who left him due to his giving up on life. Chester, re-gretfully, thought of two girls, best friends, one whom he had dated to gain access to the other, then dumped the first girl, and eventually, heartlessly, the second, although he had never captured her heart, as she was loyal to her friend.

Winston felt energy surging through his body. He knew he could heal the three young men, just as those he had healed in the last twenty-four hours. He grabbed the right hand of John, and the left hand of James. The two were so bonded in friendship, that he felt he could heal them at the same time. Both young men gasped at him, fully believing now in his powers.

"I am the once and former King of Atlantis. Upon my word, you shall be healed. So, it shall be said, so, it shall be done. You are hereby healed. Go, and serve the common good."

Peter was right next to James. He was weeping feverish-ly. His arm had regenerated from the healing energies. He had held James' left hand right before Winston had said his healing proverb.

Winston saw both John and James were now possessed of two full legs. They were barefoot. The new pink flesh was pulsating. They both passed out in disbelief and over-whelming joy. "Long Live the King!" "The common good," they both whispered as they fell into a slumber.

Winston looked at Peter.

On cue, they each wheeled one of the two men, new limbs, and all, out to the river bank, where the two made their daily pilgrimage.

Peter Taylor returned to the museum. He bought a long sleeve pullover at the gift shop. He slid his new arm through it, like he had imagined so many times in the prior months. He beamed in happiness. He tucked his right hand in for now, and returned to the group.

No one noticed him, as he stood in the back. Brooding as usual, the ladies thought.

Mary found Winston. She was smiling, but was anxious to go to the department store, as they had planned for Sunday.

Before they left, Peter had caught up to Winston and told him he was catching the next plane back to Sydney. He also exclaimed, "Long Live the King!" Winston gave him the hang five sign, and they both laughed. Soon Winston followed Mary and Elizabeth out of the museum, as they jumped on the Tube to Kensington.

The ladies walked through the revolving door and gasped at the resplendence of London's most famous department store. Smells of perfume filled the air. Winston noticed an impeccably dressed woman, likely the same age as Elizabeth, with dashing looks, at one of the counters. She was very focused, and her hair done professionally in a bun. Mary noticed her, too, and that Winston noticed her.

"Winston! Let's move on!"

The woman looked up to see the two looking at her. She figured out the fuss quickly, as she was used to men fussing over her.

"I was just admiring Britain's professional look," he responded, honestly, of course.

"I was, too. We want to see the dress department."

Winston followed them for a while before drifting to the food section of the store. He marveled at the delicious looking food, before settling in the counter for the chocolate covered fruits and nuts. He bought six. The lady behind the counter looked up at him, after he paid her with some cash. She seemed transfixed.

Winston looked around. The customers were focused on all the goodies around them. No one was paying him or the clerk any heed. He turned his stare to her. Like before, he soon saw her aura. He saw darkness emanating from her head. He saw she was suffering from Alzheimer's for some time. She had not told her employer, but knew she only had a few weeks or so left before they would know. A tear shed from her eye. She had no family. Her husband had died, and they did not have children. She had some cousins, but never saw them. The world would not miss her, she knew. But she loved her job and her customers, particularly, an elderly widowed man, who had recently paid her some attention on a daily basis.

Winston felt energy welling up inside him. He had heard her thoughts. He sensed the older gentleman was in the store, and biding his time to see her. Today was the day he would have the courage to talk to her, on a more personal level. Winston grabbed her hands. She trembled in anticipation. It was as if she knew what might be coming.

The elder man soon appeared. Winston looked too young to be flirting with his dear Abigail. He was slightly concerned, but not really.

"I am the once and former King of Atlantis. Upon my word, you shall be healed. So, it shall be said, so, it shall be done. You are hereby healed. Go, and serve the common good."

"Long Live the King!" she cried out, collapsing to her seat.

The elder man rushed over. He looked at Winston with a scowl, but when Abigail regained her composure and posture and stood ever so tall, he cracked an ever so small smile in Winston's direction.

"I am Abigail, of Chelsea, how do you do?" she beamed. She knew the darkness was gone. Her mind was sharp. She even felt younger.

"I am Charles of North Hampton. You look dazzling today. I could swear you look ten years younger. Might I not be accused of cradle snatching? And your friend?"

Charles turned around. Winston was gone.

"Why did you say Long Live the King? Has something happened to my second cousin, Queen Elizabeth?"

"Oh god, no! Shall we have some tea?" Abigail was beaming. A cousin to royalty! But she was quite wealthy herself. Her husband had made millions in shipping, and sold his company just a year before he died. *Maybe he knows who I am. I have been incognito here for three years, and have never looked like my old self, until maybe now. We shall see!*

Winston and his two ladies, left for Hyde Park. Elizabeth wanted to go to Kensington Palace, to see the Lady Di dresses. Mary wanted to see them as well. Winston took the opportunity to enjoy the ambience and spirits of former Kings and Queens in Kensington Palace. *It is as if I can feel their presence! But I have been here before, or maybe will be in the future. I feel energy here.*

Winston told his ladies he would let them take their time in the Lady Di exhibit. He walked out to Hyde Park. It was enormous. The large pond was breathtaking. Kites were being flown in the breeze. Children were shouting in playful tones. But he saw four children, two girls and two boys, maybe nine years old, sitting with appeared to be two nurses. They all looked sickly. He soon saw their aura, and knew they were terminally ill. A children's hospital was nearby. A beautiful sunny day, a picnic in the park. He saw the four wheel-chairs. The kids were not ambulatory.

Again, he felt energy welling up inside him. He saw puffy white clouds that looked like the Temple and Palace in Atlantis. He felt happiness that he might be of assistance to some kids. He then saw four mothers under the shade of a large oak tree. They were somber, but passing time with idle chatter, waiting for the end.

The kids seemed to sense his energy and presence. They gazed at him as he walked closer, in gray shorts and matching Puma gray walking sneakers. A red golf shirt against the blue sky and white clouds made him look American, especially with his white golf hat. Most London men did not wear golf or baseball caps. They saw a quickened pace, and a bounce to his step. His broad smile with straight white teeth, made him look angelic.

"Is he our guardian angel?" a little girl said to the other three kids.

One of the nurses looked on, and saw the kids watching this American gentleman approach.

"Glorious day in the park, my little friends! Would you all like to glimpse a little heaven today?"

Nurse Wanda was stunned. She saw the white aura of Winston, and dropped to her knees. The other nurse, named Beatrice, was startled and protectively put her arms around two of the kids.

"All of you hold hands with me," he said. Nurse Wanda placed her hands on the shoulders of the two children not held by the other nurse. The Nurse Beatrice, released her grip, and placed her hands on the children's shoulders like Nurse Wanda did.

"I am the once and former King of Atlantis. Upon my word, you shall be healed. So, it shall be said, so, it shall be

done. You are hereby healed. Go, and serve the common good."

The four kids giggled and laughed. Nurse Wanda passed out. Her aching back no longer ached. The ravaging acne of Nurse Beatrice, she saw, was no longer there, replaced with the porcelain skin of a doll. The Nurse Beatrice started laughing uncontrollably. She felt tears gushing from her eyes. She felt her smooth face. She trembled.

"Long Live the King!" she yelled.

The kids giggled some more and in unison shouted out, "Long Live the King!"

Winston fist pumped all four kids. He held Nurse Wanda's hands and pulled her up into a comfortable sitting position.

"You no longer have vein issues with your legs either!" he advised her with his ever-gleaming smile.

"Are you an angel? Our guardian angel?" the kids asked in unison.

"Maybe, but I think, I am just a former King!"

With that Winston headed back to Kensington Palace.

A young girl nearby soon dashed to the spot with four laughing, giggling kids. She started laughing with them. Soon two young boys and another girl joined them. They all chanted "Long Live the King!" The five kids who joined them knew not why the cheer was made, but gladly joined in the fun chorus.

The first girl yelled out, "Let's fly my kite!" All nine kids jumped up and ran to her picnic blanket, where her kite was lying, waiting to please and bounce and jump around the sky for the adoring kids.

"We are walking and running! Oh, my God! Long Live the King!" one boy shouted.

"I am so pretty again!" another chimed in, as she grabbed the kite and let her fly.

"I can fly just like the kite," the second boy cheerfully shouted.

"I am a Princess!" the second girl giggled, curling her now very curly, and newly grown blonde locks that suddenly dropped from her head as she hurled her scarf into the wind. The other girl tossed her scarf, too, feeling the breeze catch her knew dark locks as it unfurled the kite into the air. The five kids that joined them were in awe, not knowing what was going on. They let the four kids glow in happiness, and they fed off that energy.

One of the four mothers looked over at the picnic blanket. She saw the two nurses holding arms, but there were no kids. She followed the gaze of the nurses in a linear path to the nine frolicking children. There she saw what appeared to be her son, but he was not frail, and he had red hair sparkling in the sun. He had taken off his shirt, and looked like a young football player. But she saw his eyes, and buckled in a joyful fright, and collapsed into the arms of another mother.

The other two mothers soon made the same connection. They bolted full speed towards the children, screaming hysterically. The third mother slapped the face of her fallen friend. She awoke, and together they dashed towards the children. The sprint was Olympian. The four mothers would all garner a gold medal for their speed and love towards the finish line.

One by one the mothers grabbed their child and hugged them with powerful, loving hugs. The other five children backed away and watched in awe. They did not know what to do, but blurted out, "Long Live the King! Long Live the King!"

The mothers not knowing any better joined the chant, as did the newly enlivened children.

"What a miraculous day!" Nurse Wanda cheered, suddenly, adorned with a pair of shorts, that had been hidden by her sweat pants. She admired the smoothness of her suddenly golden tanned legs. They always had been shapely, she thought.

"He was our guardian angel!"

"No, he was the King!"

The kids laughed some more, and the first girl got the kite into the air. All of them watched in amazement, as the kite seemed to have come to life with tremendous animation.

Soon the healthy young children beckoned their mothers, and now a small army of other children to go to the London Eye. They took the tube, and eventually all boarded the slow-moving Ferris wheel. Over and over they chanted, "Long Live the King!" They raised their hands in the air on each rendition. Bystanders watched, uncertain as to the chant's meaning. But the kids were joyous, even the ones not sure of the chant themselves, other than that there was some sort of magician, or guardian angel that may have touched the lives so profoundly of their new-found friends.

Meanwhile, over in Central London, on the southern bank of the Thames River, John Chester Jones and James Tudor awakened from their slumber. They arose from their wheel chairs and pushed them aside forever.

"Long Live the King!" they repeatedly shouted in exuberance. The phase was catchy, and a few passersby joined them in a chant. Soon the chant died down. The two hugged each other, and went their separate ways. Each had a mission in mind for their next steps in life.

It was late afternoon. Elizabeth told her parents the next stop before going home.

"Let's stop in Camden. Wild and very different. You may smell some weed!" She laughed, waiting for a reaction.

"It is legal in many states now!" Mary exclaimed.

They took the tube to Camden. As expected, the crowd was different, but playful and energetic. It didn't take long for Winston to feel energy welling up inside of him again. Powerful energy, as it was before. He saw white billowy clouds again. He looked everywhere for auras in need of help. Soon he saw his next patient, he thought of them. A man of forty, with haggard looks, that made him look almost seventy. The man was singing and playing a guitar. His guitar box was open, but only a few pounds had made their way to his box. He looked up as Winston approached. Mary and Elizabeth had strolled ahead, and expected that Winston would be slow to keep up. So, they marched forward.

The guitar man stopped playing and gazed up at Winston. His eyes were blurry from alcohol, cannabis and a hard life. He felt the winds of high octane energy blowing in his direction. Winston seemed to glow white to him. He saw billowy white clouds, too. And they seemed to spell out musical notes. With trembling hands, he reached out to hold the extended hand of Winston.

"I am the once and former King of Atlantis. Upon my word, you shall be healed. So, it shall be said, so, it shall be done. You are hereby healed. Go, and serve the common good."

"Long Live the King!" the guitar man shouted.

He felt younger and healthier than he had in years. His vision and mind were clear. He was refreshed and sober. He laughed loudly. His black skin glistened, and he howled in delight. Slowly, the musical notes of the clouds formed the notes of a new song for him. New lyrics arrived, too. He experimented and practiced his new-found vision from the clouds. Winston winked and left. Soon guitar man was belting out his new song. Dozens flocked to listen and add many pounds to his guitar box. "Long Live the King!" He shouted as he finished. The crowd returned the chant with enthusiasm.

Mary saw Winston panting as he finally caught them.

"I have had enough. Let's go back to Southwark and prepare for the play."

"Yes, let's do that," he huffed.

6.

WINSTON SAID nothing on the Tube ride back to Central London. The energy that had flowed through him that day had zapped him of much of his own energy. He was happy to return to Elizabeth's flat to recharge.

"I will nap for a tad. You two can take your time getting ready for the play tonight at the Playhouse! Romeo and Juliet! Elizabeth, who is your Romeo?" Winston teased, his eyebrows mischievously raised.

"Daddy, you know I am not seeing anyone special right now!" Elizabeth frowned, and bounce up the stairs. *Does he know something?*

Mary follower her, and looked upon her wardrobe she had packed. There were still a couple of outfits she had not worn. Certainly, a colorful Lily dress would hit the spot for a play!

Elizabeth wore a bright flowered dress, to keep up with her Mum. Winston put on a blazer over his tan slacks. He put on some leather shoes, dropping his Nike walking shoes to the floor in retirement for the day.

Together they sauntered to the Playhouse. The play was sold out. They took their refreshments, and mingled with the other patrons. Soon they all took their seats to watch Romeo and Juliet.

The play was captivating and all watched with great enthusiasm, even though they all knew the plot and characters by heart. Winston was passive for the first part of the performance. But he was overwhelmed with auras again as the second part to the play began. He soon saw so many maladies and broken auras. He felt restricted by the large crowd. He knew innately that his healing must remain unpublicized, or else mass hysteria could evolve, at least in his own mind. Floods of people demanding to be healed of any and all maladies and ailments. Or demanding financial benefits or personal favors, or success in sports. But his heart tugged at him to help.

Soon the play ended. As the actors held hands to accept applause, the lead actor and actress glanced at Winston, winked, and spoke to the adoring patrons.

"Let us all hold hands. You on the aisles hold the hand of the person behind you or in front of you so that we all are connected as one!" the two actors belted out in their powerful voices, shaking beneath their costumes, and perspiring beneath their make-up.

The patrons struggled at first to comprehend and execute the odd command, but some boisterous few shouted out, "We are one!" The theatre personnel grasped the command and helped in its eventual execution. The patrons all chanted, "We are one!"

Winston felt the most energy he had ever felt roar from inside him. He even saw his own aura leaping high from his body. Some in the crowd noticed, but because they did not possibly appreciate what they were seeing, disregarded the light as background light from the stage, or a reflection.

"I am the once and former King of Atlantis. Upon my word, you shall be healed. So, it shall be said, so, it shall be

done. You are hereby healed. Go, and serve the common good," Winston belted out.

No one heard him above the din. Elizabeth heard some words about the common good, and slapped him five, as hands separated from hands across the theater. All felt the energy. But it was just the exhilaration of cheering with their fellow patrons, like cheering with fellow fans at a football game on a game winning goal. It was a powerful common bond. Not a bond one forgot readily.

The buzz slowed down. The patrons filed out dutifully in order. The two actors then belted out, "Long Live the King!"

A few patrons reiterated the chant, not knowing its whereabouts, but assuming it was a reference to the King of ancient times during the time of Shakespeare perhaps.

But as they left, a wonderful invisible mist enveloped the patrons. It was magnificent in feeling and its presence. They all smiled and laughed, unknowing of their new-found freedom from physical and mental infirmities. One elder man tossed his cane into the trash bin. A few others roared in assent and tossed canes aside, too. A man who had suffered a stroke and wore a brace for his drop step watched in awe. He bent over and removed his brace. Surprisingly, his foot no longer dropped. He had full maneuverability of his ankle and foot. He grabbed his wife and hugged her tightly. He noticed his pain from osteo and rheumatoid arthritis had disappeared as well. His wife kissed him very deeply, more deeply than in years. He noticed she was leaning hard on her right leg. Her right hip must be better he thought.

Another man felt his upper left chest. A familiar bump was missing. He could not believe it. His pace maker was gone. He felt great. His heart was racing in excitement, but normally. He knew his fibrillation was gone. He kissed his wife in total passion. They momentarily blocked the aisle as the patient patrons behind them applauded in enthusiasm.

More and more couples embraced in passionate hugs and kisses. Older folks were equally enamored with their loved ones, as the youthful players at the play.

"We are one! Long Live the King!" they suddenly chanted over and over, combining the two earlier chants. The actor and actress looked down from the stage and bowed one final time. They embraced and kissed themselves. They saw Winston. The plan had worked. But they were discreet. Even without orders from the King to be silent and secretive of his request at the final intermission, they knew to respect his anonymity. For they too had been healed during the intermission of their weak and tired backs and hips. The actress had lost her acne marks of her youth. Now even without heavy makeup, her natural beauty would shine for all to see, day and night.

The patrons poured into the Riverwalk along the River Thames. They cheered, laughed and danced into the night. Soon dozens of bystanders marveled at their fun and delight.

"Long Live the King!" began to echo up and down the Riverwalk. Some had remembered the cheer and chant from earlier in the day. Some were concerned the Queen had died. But there was nothing on their mobile devices in the news, social media or any media. Puzzlement waved through many, but soon the patrons left for their homes. One by one, as the energy from comradery and companionship with their fellow patrons disappeared, they noticed they were new persons, with healthy attitudes, healed wounds and cured maladies. They determined it was the collective power of fellow humans bonded in love and devotion, and the power of the human spirit taken to the highest levels of existence. The enormity of the night overwhelmed them, as they scurried to their beds for a night of welcomed slumber and sobriety. Surely it was only a dream, or the power of mind over matter for one glorious night, they re-thought as their heavy heads hit their collective pillows, all literally at the same time.

Included in the slumbering masses, were Winston, Mary and Elizabeth. The latter two had already been healed, so they were not aware of the true enormity of Romeo and Juliet's love, that glorious Sunday night in Central London.

7.

WINSTON AWOKE in the morning, Monday, the last day of a holiday weekend. Mary and Elizabeth were up, fully dressed, and made up for the morning gallivanting. He was stunned. He always had to wait for them to get ready. He was so slow a walker, but they were so slow to get ready.

"Winston, get ready!" Mary admonished him. She was wearing tan shorts and a long sleeve top, tight to the body, but warm, sun-reflecting, and perspiration wicking. She wore her comfortable Nike running sneakers, with the bright green swoosh. Elizabeth wore a tee shirt with her favorite football team logo on it. She wore long jeans, and her Nike running sneakers, with the bright green swoosh. She tied her very long blonde hair in a pony-tail. Mary wore a head ban, holding her shorter blonde hair in place, although still long enough for a pony tail, when needed. Winston threw on some khakis, and wore a white golf shirt, with his country club logo on it. He dawned a golf cap, as he had every day, and grabbed his sunglasses.

"Elizabeth, where are we off to, today, my young dear?" Winston asked of his daughter. Mary chirped, before Elizabeth could respond.

"Oh, Anne liked our photos from Kensington Palace and the Lady Di exhibit! She can't wait to come here to visit you, Elizabeth. I am glad you and your sister are so close!" Mary exclaimed, as she banged away more texts to her younger daughter. Elizabeth joined the fray and sent texts to her sister and some of her friends, as well as some Instagrams. Winston was retired. He looked at his emails, just a few of his golf buddies setting up tee times for his return on Thursday. This was their second to last day in London. They would fly out from Heathrow early on Wednesday. Soon the social media sharing and communications came to a halt. The ladies were ready.

"Off to Primrose today, Father. You will like it. I have a surprise of sorts for you!"

And off they went on the Tube. Winston had temporarily forgotten his healing wizardry and accomplishments, his Kingdom in Atlantis, his life in what seemed like another dimension, world, universe or realm. But the memories slowly seeped through to his consciousness. At first it was just the memories of early morning dreaming, where the memories of daily events jumbled together in life like movies, that were enjoyable to watch and when recalled, fun to remember and even more challenging to decipher. But he jolted to attention when the flood of memories of the play, and then the museum, and then the Riverwalk, the department store, Hyde Park, Camden, not in any sequential order, burst forth like a powerful river flood. The memories were real, not dreams. He recalled all the healing actions with clarity. He started to breathe heavily, and hyperventilate. Mary was shocked into attention to her husband. She thought he was having a serious attack and feared the worst.

"Winston!" she shouted, holding his head up and his face in her hands.

Winston was shocked back to normal. His breathing slowed.

"Should we take him to the hospital!" Elizabeth cried out, so concerned for her deeply loved father.

Winston took control of himself. He calmed himself down, almost instantly.

"I feel fine now. I am ok. It was just a dream that overwhelmed me, one from last night! I am fine, I do believe," Winston said solemnly, rubbing his eyes, and then meeting Mary's eyes.

Should I tell them. They have not really said much about how their maladies and ailments are gone. Why did they not share that with me? They keep so many secrets from me. Maybe that is the answer. Protect them from this craziness. AH, I love them so. No need for them to be burdened by the pressure that may come to heal so many.

They arrived at the Primrose station in north London. Elizabeth said, "Follow me, dear Mum and Dad."

They passed by a street with homes that were brightly colored in pastel pink, yellow or blue. Mary and Elizabeth took many selfies up and down the street. Winston admired the homes, but stayed back and simply enjoyed the laughter of his wife and daughter. He texted Anne, and wished her good luck in her adult league field hockey game back in Boston. A few emoji later he turned his focus back to the present place.

"Now, Dad, here we go!"

Elizabeth grabbed both of her parents by the hand on either side of her, and started to skip up the sidewalk. Soon they had arrived at Primrose Park. Up the tall hill they skipped, with Winston and Mary breathlessly keeping up. At last they reached the top of the hill.

"Whoa!"

"Oh, me!"

Her parents were stunned by the magnificent beauty of the unobstructed view of the London skyline. The three of them took in the view with awe, and said nothing for a few moments. Below, they watched many children flying kites, and playing Frisbee or catch. It was a holiday, so kids were not in school on this Monday. Elizabeth saw two teenage girls playing catch with lacrosse sticks, much to her delight, as she had played in college. Dogs gallivanted around without a care in total freedom and delight. Wine, Primm's and ale were aplenty. The sun-splashed day was magnificent. The sky was pure blue with no smog or humidity. The temperature was warm enough that sweaters and light jackets were lying in heaps all around.

They walked down the hill and enjoyed the conviviality of all around them. Happiness was aplenty.

Soon they left the park. Winston had not seen any auras. He wondered if his reversion back to his Atlantean soul had retired or gone into a suspended state. He was relieved it was over, at least for now. He saw no clouds. The sky was cloudless.

They headed out. Suddenly, there was a terrible bang. It jolted Winston. He had fallen behind. It was on the street with the multi-colored homes. He heard a scream, and then silence. He looked into the sky. There were two tiny clouds. His walk turned into a sprint. He saw an elderly woman with a scarf running from the porch of her pink colored home.

"Help! Please, Help!"

He saw her calling for emergency services. NO sirens heard, yet.

He dashed to the scene. There were twin little girls pinned to the sidewalk by the car on top of them, their bones crushed, conscious and freaking out in pain and total unbridled fear. Winston saw their auras. Their spirits were barely clinging on to their crushed bodies. In the car, he saw a very elderly woman. She appeared lifeless, he thought. She had suffered a massive coronary. But then he saw her eyes open. She pleaded to him to save the girls. She clung to life by a thin thread to watch to see if Winston could save the little girls. Her metaphysical heart was crushed in sadness and horror, more painful than the coronary. The elderly woman with the scarf saw Winston's blue eyes, shining brightly from the sky. A calmness gripped her. It was if she knew.

Winston told her to back the car away from the sidewalk pavement. The elderly woman with the scarf pushed the driver, her ninety-old cousin, aside and reversed the car away from the sidewalk. The crunch of bones was excruciatingly painful to hear. The girls were her granddaughters. Winston bent over and held each of the girl's hands, as they shrieked even louder in pain. He heard the approaching sirens.

"I am the once and former King of Atlantis. Upon my word, you shall be healed. So, it shall be said, so, it shall be done. You are hereby healed. Go, and serve the common good."

Instantly, the two girls opened their hazel colored eyes. Their bloody screams were silenced. Their eyelashes flitted in shock, and then calmness. Their sandy brown hair was no longer crusted with crimson from their blood. Winston watched their spirits reattach firmly inside them. They stood.

"Long Live the King!" They cried out and hugged him at the same time. The elderly woman with the scarf quietly sang out, "Long Live the King!" She then passed out. Winston walked to the car. He leaned inside. He gazed into the dying eyes of the elderly woman. She said "Let me pass. I am ready."

The two girls ran to the aid of their grandmother, one of the great dames of British society, Grace Bennington. The grandmother awoke quickly and wept in sadness. She looked over and saw her cousin was gone. The ambulance driver arrived and looked at her cousin. He tested her for vital signs. He tried to revive her, to no avail. He then closed her eyes, and covered her face with a sheet as she was wheeled off in a gurney and loaded onto the ambulance.

The girls, Starr and Sensa, were fine, but trembling at the memory of their near-death experience. The grandmother bent over and held her toddler granddaughters, and together they cried, and then smiled as they watched a large white cloud pass over them. They all swore it was her cousin, with the broadest of smiles. They then looked at Winston. One of the girls ran and hugged him on his leg. The twin joined her. He patted them on the head.

"Lead a strong and clean life! God bless!"

Winston winked at the grandmother, her scarf now held in her hand, her long gray hair uncoiled down her shoulders and back.

"Thank you, thank you forever!"

"She wanted to go."

"I know," she said.

Winston headed back to the main street to find Mary and Elizabeth.

"Did you see what was the commotion?"

"Indeed, I did. A car crashed up on a sidewalk. It looked like the driver may not have made it. An elderly woman. She had a smile on her face, though," Winston said, with a blank stare.

The three of them headed back to the tube after grabbing a quick snack from a street vendor. Winston watched the kites play in the sky, as a lonely cloud peered down. Off to the Tube, and off to Greenwich.

Soon they reached Greenwich. Winston had wanted to see the CuttySark. It was magnificent in its beauty and rich in history. The fastest boat ever of its kind, it now rested in the harbor here for all to admire and touch and see.

Soon they trekked up the long steep hill to see the prime meridian, the vertical equivalent of the equator. As they walked they watched two dogs running with full speed up and down the grassy fields. They were in full fun mode, free to roam and chase each other.

"Oh! Look. That is so sad!" Elizabeth pointed to a third dog missing it rear left leg. It, too, watched the two dogs galloping through the park. It whined in sadness, wanting to join the fun. It would attempt to follow, only to fall to the ground after reaching any kind of speed. The two running dogs were of different sizes, and both a pure-bred. One was a golden retriever, well-groomed and cared for. The pursuing dog was a small Shih-Tzu. It scampered so quickly, the golden retriever had to use its superior speed to evade its playful snapping of his pursuer's jaws. The three-legged dog was a mutt. It had lost its leg while chasing a ball from its owner's daughter. Mother and daughter were sad watching Jackson, his name, wince in pain on every fall.

Winston fell behind again. Elizabeth and Mary both ran 10K races on a regular basis, and were soldiers in the gym, and masters of the stair-masters and elliptical. Winston walked when he golfed, but not much else.

Winston thought of the two girls. *I think they were twins. I guess I still am in the paranormal zone. It looks like I really was a healer and a King in a remote past. I should embrace this.*

Energy welled inside him again. He saw the aura of the Mum and her daughter. He saw their empathy and love for their doggy. Soon the doggy stopped pining to play with the two running dogs. It hopped away from its masters towards Winston. It reached Winston and stopped, resting awkwardly on its one rear haunch. Its tongue hung sideways from its mouth and its tail wagged against the sidewalk pavement. Its big brown eyes, surrounded by its brown and white furry face, just locked into Winston's eyes. Mum and daughter were distracted, eyeing a thunderstorm fast approaching, with the wind picking up with some surprising momentum.

Winston bent over, and smiled at his new canine friend. He grabbed its two paws.

"I am the once and former King of Atlantis. Upon my word, you shall be healed. So, it shall be said, so, it shall be done. You are hereby healed. Go, and serve the common good, your masters and your two new dog friends."

The dog, Jackson, knew he was free. The chains and bondage were gone. He leapt up and licked Winston on the face, and dashed away after the golden retriever. The Shih-Tzu rolled over four times in the soft grass, as Jackson nudged her playfully away to take the lead in the chase. Jackson caught the surprised golden, who immediately bowed down and sniffed and checked out a new friend. The Shih-Tzu soon joined them and they playfully frolicked and rolled around in the grassy field, nipping and barking at each other.

"Oh, my God!" Elizabeth shrieked. She loved animals. Every time there was a commercial on television with the faces of poor animals in Africa or kennels or shelters, she would take down the number and email address, and make the yearly donations. "Mum, Dad, look the little dog is running! It has its leg back! What is going on!! It is a miracle! It is so happy!" She cried, with real tears streaming down her cheeks.

Mother and daughter heard the screams and words of Elizabeth. They turned to see Jackson running full steam at them. Jackson hurtled into the air into the waiting arms of the daughter, knocking her to the ground and endlessly licking her on the face. She wept in joy. Her Mum cried, too, not comprehending the enormity of the miracle.

The thunder boomed and lightning struck nearby.

"It must have been the lightning or the energy from the lightning!" The daughter yelled, as her mother hurried her to the shelter of the ship museum below.

Elizabeth wanted to pat the dog in the worst way. "Oh!"

But Mary grabbed her and caught up with Winston. A maintenance vehicle came by. The three of them jumped aboard, and the driver headed the vehicle in the other direction to the museum on top of the hill, where the prime meridian mark was located.

"Daddy! Did you see that? The dog grew back its missing leg!!" Elizabeth shouted out.

"Indeed! Maybe a miracle! Maybe the lightning, like the girl said," he mustered a response.

Winston felt the power of the energy of the storm. It was as if the energy was attracted to him. Or maybe it was attracted the source of his energy. Another bolt struck a nearby tree, and split it in half. The energy radiated away and struck Winston as if he were a magnet. His hair stood straight into the air, and his limbs tingled. He thought he was dying. The vehicle tipped over and all three of them tumbled down the hill. The driver was under the cart. Another bolt hit yet another tree. The water poured from the sky, and then hail.

"Leave me here! Go to the ship museum now!!" Winston belted out as loud as he could. His leg was broken, and he could not stand up.

"I will take care of the driver and call for help. GO NOW!

Mary and Elizabeth were frightened out of their wits. Mary had never liked thunder. Her Uncle had been killed on a golf course by lightning, and she feared it with deep dread. Elizabeth was fearless, assumed her brave Dad was fine, and grabbed her anxious uncontrollably freaking out Mum, and half carried and half slid down the grassy banks and fields. A museum guard had come out to assist, and Elizabeth and the guard carried Mary inside the museum.

"I must return to get Dad!" Elizabeth shouted.

"No!" said the museum guard. The lightning is upon us. I saw the bolt. I think it hit your father and the driver. I have called in emergency services. They will be here shortly. The storm is a short and intense burst. It will be gone in minutes. It has caused much destruction in its path. There is a tornado, too."

Elizabeth turned pale. She was fearless, except for tornados. She cowered into her Mum's arms. Her Mum was of no help. She was shaking in fear and cold.

Winston lay there. He saw his leg was broken and his right arm singed. He felt enormous pain and burning. He saw his own aura leaping away from him.

Maybe this is the end. What a way to pass. I have healed so many. Is it a blessing?

But then he saw the driver. He had been hit directly by the bolt bending off of the fallen and split tree. He was barely breathing, his flesh smoldering. Even if he lived, he would be in burn units for years, and his face was gone.

Winston restrained the flow of energy. He felt it was a magnet to him. He had to wait for the lightning and thunder to pass. It was his fault the driver was near death. Hopefully, the driver would survive long enough until the storm passed, but before emergency services arrived and took them both away. The hail bruised him everywhere. *This is a punishing final moment on earth.*

The driver was perilously close to a departure to another realm. Winston dragged his heavy, wet, and limp body next to the driver. He heard sirens. Another crack of lightning nearby. He felt his body reverberate in the energy flow. It ran right through him. He clutched the hands of the driver, all the hair burned away. He took a big risk. His act of healing might also deliver a fateful blow to the driver and him, and possibly the two emergency workers scampering up the hill.

"I am the once and former King of Atlantis. Upon my word, you shall be healed. So, it shall be said, so, it shall be done. You are hereby healed. Go, and serve the common good."

Another bolt of lightning struck as the healing energy from Winston transfused through the driver's body. The energy from the bolt was tamed by Winston's powerful spirit and then harnessed to heal himself as well. The rest of the bolt passed harmlessly into the ground. Winston in his temporary enormous strength, had moved the vehicle off of the driver.

The two emergency workers arrived, ready to serve the victims of the storm. The driver had stood instantaneously, aided by the power of the bolt. Winston was on his back, breathing heavily. The workers checked his vital signs. He was alive! His heart was pumping at 160 beats a minute, the highest ever. But soon it slowed.

"We are fine!" The driver shouted. "I feel enlightened!"

"Long Live the King!"

The workers repeated the chant. One had heard rumors of healing and the accompanying chant. He gazed at Winston.

"Come here my friend." The worker had been terribly burned in an apartment fire a couple of years ago, and had lost hearing in his left ear from an explosion while he was in the building. He had saved four children from the fire, and was thought of as a hero. But it was his job to save people. He did not consider himself a hero.

Winston grabbed his hands.

"I am the once and former King of Atlantis. Upon my word, you shall be healed. So, it shall be said, so, it shall be done. You are hereby healed. Go, and continue to serve the common good."

The worker fell to his knees and wept. He heard the thunder now from a distance with both of his ears. He knew the burn injuries would be gone, but wanted to wait to go home with his wife to share the miracle and the joy. He gazed up at Winston.

"Long Live the King!"

Winston saw the sun now poke its head out, snarling at the departing storm burst.

"You both are faithful servants of the common good. May you have peace and happiness the rest of your days."

Winston slapped the vehicle driver's hand in a high five. The emergency workers joined suit.

"I have no formal education beyond high school, but I am sure I am a genius now!" He laughed.

Winston left the three of them. Down below he slogged into the ship museum. He found Elizabeth talking to a Mum and daughter.

"Dad! What happened to your hair! Its grown back!! What the heck!"

"I was struck by lightning! Maybe that did it! I don't know. Are you sure?" Winston hesitated to say more.

"It must be the lightning. Look, my dog Jackson, he now has his leg back! It is a miracle!" The daughter said.

"Oh, he is so cute!" Elizabeth cooed.

"We must go, I am so tired," Winston proclaimed, his head slouching forward, as usual. He put his hat on to cover his new hair. Elizabeth forgot about his hair, as she petted Jackson vigorously before they departed.

On the Tube again, back to Southwark, they went.

Another incredible day. When will it stop. I wonder. Yes, it is a wonder.

Winston crashed when they got back to the flat. Mary and Elizabeth showered and put on warm and dry clothes.

"Should Dad go to the hospital?

"The medics let him go, so he must be fine. Let us check him in the morning," Mary replied, still startled at the day's events, and dumbfounded at the lightning caused miracles. She felt her heart beat. Still no pain.

8.

WINSTON AWOKE early that Tuesday morning. He recalled no dreams. He hustled to the bathroom. Sure enough. He had a full head of hair. It was not long. He wondered how Elizabeth noticed. He wondered why Mary said nothing. He wondered if the lightning hit knocked her circuits haywire. He would monitor her closely. He took his electric razor and cut his new hair down. Now, it looked normal.

He decided to take a walk and get some iced green tea. He bought some tea with a lemon wedge, and a blueberry scone. He decided to walk down to the river. He turned right to the East. It was as if he was being summoned. He saw the man with no hunch on his back. He would always remember his eyes.

"Hail to the King!" the man saluted him. Together they walked toward Tower Bridge.

"I am eternally grateful to you for healing me. I have spent the last waking hours of my two days since you healed me serving the common good. I volunteered up at the children's hospital, reading to them and helping the parents find lodging and food establishments. I helped four of my fellow homeless friends hook up with some shelters. I even found some employment at a coffee shop for another homeless woman. I tried to heal them using your chant, to no avail! I am not a King like you! One of the nurses said I could apply for a job at the hospital for room and board, and a small stipend. I even think she may like me. There was a reporter from the London's leading newspaper asking a lot of questions about the King and the rumored healing. She seemed to know he was possibly an American, white and over sixty. No one offered her any insight, other than musings that they may have heard something. She blurted out to one person that the Queen was alive and well! I, of course, will keep your cover! My senses are heightened. I feel you are being called out today. May I walk with you. Even to see another healing miracle would be so energizing."

Winston listened intently. "Does the reporter have a name?"

"Yes, she introduced herself repeatedly to her targets. Her name was Becca Hollingsworth. She was tall, slender, attractive, and very proper. I am sure she is well-educated! She dressed impeccably, even wearing high heels. Her reddish blonde hair was in a bun, and she had high cheekbones, and professional glasses covering her blue eyes. Ha! I was quite impressed, don't you think. She was maybe thirty or so years old. Still a beat reporter making her way," the man with no hunch explained, quite impressed with his forensic analysis.

"What is your name?" Winston asked.

"I was Bartholomew. You can call me Bart. Honestly, I don't recall my last name. I was always an orphan, as long as I can remember," Bart sheepishly recalled his past.

"How about Bart Starr, the name of a great American quarterback in American football?"

"Na, I don't like American football. How about Bart Tower," he decided, as he looked at Tower Bridge.

They both looked at the Bridge at the same time. They saw quite a commotion. A man was hanging over the railing. Some pedestrians on their way to work were coaxing him to return to the safety of the sidewalk. But then he jumped, flopping into the river, just missing a passing boat. The boat's captain did not see him. He submerged, and popped up momentarily.

Bart took off his shoes and coat and raced to an entrance to the beach near the river. He dove into the water head first and swam hurriedly in the direction of the tide. Many on the bridge watched helplessly. He took a line ahead of the place he lost saw the man. Winston had run to the beach, and kept pace by foot.

Bart finally reached the man. He had been knocked out by the fall, and was drowning. Bart grabbed him under the shoulders and held his head above water. He kicked hard with his feet and pulled water with his free right hand. He gulped water on the way. Soon he brought the man to shore. Passersby watched from the sidewalk behind the railings. Winston slammed the back of Bart to knock water from his lungs. Bart then pumped water from the chest of the dying man. He gave him CPR and mouth to mouth resuscitation. Soon the man coughed and woke up.

The man stared at Bart.

"You saved me. But I was trying to go away from this life. I wanted to pass on," the man cried.

Winston looked on. The man was going to live. Bart had saved him. Bart was a star disciple, for sure.

Winston tapped Bart on the shoulder. "You have served the common good! May your remaining days be prosperous and peaceful. I will let you attend to this man and his life."

Winston left the scene. He could hear Bart counseling the man on his life. He then heard them both chant, "Long Live the King!"

Bart ran after him. "There is a young girl, maybe five, who is terminally ill. She is an orphan like I was. Would you heal her? I can bring her out tonight at 8:00 P.M. at my bench?" Bart cried, knowing he was begging for help.

"Sure Bart. I will be there."

Winston returned to the flat. Mary and Elizabeth were waiting for him. Off to Windsor Castle for the day.

"The Queen is there today!" Mary noted.

Winston said nothing.

They stopped in Notting Hill for a delicious breakfast outside an elegant café. They each had salmon, poached eggs, and an avocado mixture that was divine. After the breakfast, they went to see a few shops on Portobello. Mary bought some trinkets, and Elizabeth a nice sun hat. Finally, they took the Tube back to the train stop for Windsor.

In no time, they had made it to Windsor. They first took the long walk in front of the Castle all the way to the end and back. The line had diminished when they returned. Soon they were in the Castle, with its former moats, and tall inner Castle on the hill. The Queen was there, as they saw her flag.

They visited the doll house exhibit, and walked endlessly through the hallways of countless paintings of former Kings and Queens and other nobles. Winston recalled Winchester Abby, where some of these very Kings and Queens rested in peace. His Kingdom was long before England had ever established its sovereignty.

He felt a presence. His energy level was normal. He wondered if it was the Queen.

The Queen was in her office. Her secretary was in the room.

"What is this rumor that chants of 'Long Live the King!' are rampant though out the city? Do they want to abdicate my throne? My second cousin called me to make sure I was all right. He would not tell me more. But he is engaged to be married at his ripe old age. I shall meet her soon. We should have a small gala for them."

"The chants do not have to do with you. Our intelligence says a man saying is a former King is healing people. No one will talk. I heard the number one beat reporter from London's leading newspaper, Becca Hollingsworth, has found nothing. We are in touch with her. She had called to make sure you were alive! She had heard about the chants, particularly, after the Romeo and Juliet play at the Playhouse. I would not be concerned. Certainly, he is not an English King," her secretary concluded, brushing her light wool suit, to free it of non-existent wrinkles.

"I sense a strong presence. You don't suppose he may be near today, or God knowing, in my Castle. Maybe he could return my youth! I could live to the century mark and beyond. What does he look like?"

"No one has said. A man was saved near the Tower Bridge today. A man in his forties dove into the river and saved him. There were some chants of 'Long Live the King!', so maybe he is our healing King. Both the survivor and his savior disappeared before the police could investigate. Another older man was nearby, possibly in his sixties. Maybe he is the King."

"Mingle in the crowd. Maybe he is here. If someone is healed, maybe we can flush him out. Maybe you should say I have taken ill! Maybe he will want to be a knight in shining armor to save me. Never mind on that. Silly idea."

"I will walk around. Most of the people hear are older than sixty this time of week. He is white and wears a cap, if he is the older gentleman. If he is the younger gentleman, he had dark hair. Not much to go on. I will let you know. Only if the chants happen will we know!"

Winston was in the same wing now as the Queen. He knew he felt her presence, because he overheard she was upstairs in her office. He felt a strong tug just to walk upstairs to meet her. He simply walked to a guard and said, "The Queen is expecting me."

"What is your name sir?" the guard said, while secretly calling other security officers over.

"I am the King."

The guard looked at him, and then two security guards escorted him out of the building. After searching him, they led him to the exit. He simply went to a pub and had a burger. He texted Mary where he was, and within an hour, she and Elizabeth had joined him. They each ordered draft ale, and soon gobbled down some burgers, as well. Finally, they left for the river.

Mary wanted to take the short river cruise. They boarded the boat, and soon were on a guided tour. The horse track amazed them, as did the University. The countryside was so beautiful. Finally, they returned. They caught the train back to Central London.

The Queen sat down for supper. She overheard one of the guards talking to the chef. Her alarms went off, as she heard the words, 'He said he was a King'.

Instantly, she called in the guard.

"Tell me everything that happened. Why was not I apprised of this situation?" She barked at him.

"Your Grace, it was just some older retired gentleman, fancying himself a King, to garner a meeting with you. We checked him out. He was of no threat. I believe he was an American. I believe he may have been with his wife and daughter. It sounded from the conversation that the daughter lives in London, and her parents were visiting. She mentioned something about getting her in trouble at work. He tried to wave them over when we escorted him out. We later saw them leave about an hour later. You are fine!" the guard explained, nervous at the rebuke.

"Fine, carry on. Tell my secretary to see me at once."

In a few minutes her personal secretary had arrived.

"He was here! I knew I felt his presence. It was the sixty-year-old. He is an American. He was here with his wife and daughter."

"I did not hear of anyone being healed today."

The guard came in on hearing the word healed.

"Odd that you say that. But when I returned after removing the retired gentleman, I found my knee felt better. In fact, it is totally better. He was mumbling something under his breath about being a King and serving the common good. But I think I may have been healed by him," the guard concluded his statement, bowed and left the dining room.

"It is him, then. And he is a King. I wonder, where is his Kingdom. I should have gone downstairs to mingle. Maybe I would have met him. We must find him before he returns to America."

"Should I tell Becca Hollingsworth of London's leading newspaper, of this turn of events?"

"Possibly. I do trust her, but let me ponder that. But as Queen, I do want to meet this King. Leave intelligence out of this for now. He is a peaceful and healing King. He is of no threat. But you and the guard can check our video surveillance and credit card records of visitors today, to see what you can find. Carry on!"

The secretary and the guard bowed their heads and left the room. The Queen stared into space, and then a portrait of a King who died in the Fifteenth Century. *Maybe the reincarnation of Henry VIII or, what if, King Arthur himself. This is so exciting.*

The train ride home was full of hearty, drunken fans from a local rugby match. They seemed fixated on one named Chester. Over and over they sang songs and inserted Chester's names into the lyrics. "We love you Chester..." "We love you Chester..." "Chester, Chester, calling out Chester!" They kept baying until they all poured out of the train at one stop. It seemed so silent. One woman said, "We wonder which one was Chester?"

Winston and family returned to Southwark at seven thirty. All were tired. Tomorrow, they would take a flight from Heathrow to Boston, to return home to Connecticut.

Winston told them he would be back in an hour. Mary and Elizabeth suspected he was certainly shopping for one last trinket for them.

Winston had done that the day before. He hurried to the small park near London Bridge to find the bench. He arrived on time. There sitting on the bench was a little girl covered in a fresh blanket. A few steps back stood Bart Tower. No one was around.

The girl beamed a glorious smile. She must have been told of the healing powers of the King. Winston approached her, grabbed her hands and spoke his now favorite words, "I am the once and former King of Atlantis. Upon my word, you shall be healed. So, it shall be said, so, it shall be done. You are hereby healed. Go, and serve the common good."

The girl stood and raised her hands to the sky. "Long Live the King!" she rejoiced. Bart had yelled the phrase at the same time.

"Maybe you can be her foster father, Bart. That would be special. And take that job at the hospital!"

"I will, Your Grace!"

"That man today was once a wealthy man. His wife left him because of his infidelity. His two children, a son and daughter, have cut him off. He is bankrupt and penniless. His health is good, save his mental depression and anxiety.

I told him he was saved for a reason, to serve the common good. I don't know if he can be saved though."

"Tell him to return to his wife. He should not touch her finances, and shall use his extraordinary mind to serve the common good. He is creative, he will find a way."

"I shall do that. And you? You are certainly an American tourist. I know that."

"I leave tomorrow. But my daughter is here. So, I shall return. I do want to play some golf courses in Scotland."

"We have some nice courses in England, too. Don't forget London. You are now part of its fabric. You will be lore and legend! We, the healed, know to be discreet. But I don't know how long it will be before the secret breaks. Of course, I know not your legal name. Or your name as King in Atlantis."

"Thank you, Bart. I know where to find you on my return."

With that Winston said good-bye. He hugged the little girl and Bart. He walked home to the flat.

The next morning Winston and Mary boarded their flight to Boston. Winston did not heal anyone that day. He was fine with that. He wondered if his healing powers would work in America.

9.

ECCA SAT at her desk, early Wednesday morning. She read the story of the man saved near the Tower Bridge. She was puzzled but infinitely curious. It was the mention of a sixty-year-old near the scene that sounded the alarm bells. She hustled down to the office of the reporter. He was not there. She texted him. He told her he was not there. He had compiled his reports based on reports over social media.

She took her light coat and determined she would head back to Southwark, where so many rumored events had occurred. She grabbed the Tube, and turned on her smartphone device. She scrolled down all the latest stories. She searched for King, for healing. Nothing came up. One story captured her interest. A local man in Greenwich has won ten million pounds in the lottery. He claimed he had been struck by lightning, and that he became a genius. He claimed the lightning brought him the numbers from above. He told the press he would serve the common good. He was a maintenance worker from the park at Greenwich surrounding the Prime Meridian. He said another man had been struck by lightning, too, and maybe a dog. He hoped they were well.

Becca scribbled down some notes in her notebook on her smartphone. "Check emergency services for last few days up in Greenwich."

She finally arrived at Southwark. She strolled up the Riverwalk. The people seemed ordinary, and in no hurry. There was a peaceful ambience. The day was cloudy, a bit cool, but there was no rain. The breeze was brisk, and small white caps could be seen on the river. She would not take water transportation home, as she was susceptible to motion sickness. She pulled her collar up to protect her neck from the breeze. Soon she approached London Bridge. By happenstance, she glanced over at the small park. She saw a park bench. She strolled over and sat down on the bench and just stared at the river.

This is such a puzzle. Why are people chanting "Long Live the King!" Have people been healed. So many rumors.

She then cast her eyes away and saw a trash bin. She could see into the bin, as the sides were made of an aluminum mesh. She saw a jersey that looked to be a patient's jersey. She walked over and pulled it out. It appeared to be the smock of a young child.

Could it be a child who was healed?

She called a few hospitals, asking about children who may have suddenly healed, or gone into remission. All claimed privacy laws. But she sensed nothing was there. She searched news sites. Nothing. But then again, one administrator seemed to waffle, or even equivocate, somewhat. A visit there tomorrow, too, she thought. Or a follow-up call today to a nurse or other worker.

A graduate of Oxford, she was well schooled. She wanted to be a reporter. She had turned down some promotions, to stay as a reporter. She authored children's books in her spare time, one series of which had provided her with a steady stream of passive income. She felt her investigative skills here were not working very well. The day before she had asked everyone if they had seen the healer, or the King. No one gave her any indication or evidence that they had.

She called emergency services. A person answered.

"Yes, we did dispatch an ambulance to the park in Greenwich. There were no casualties reported by our medics. A driver of a maintenance cart and a passenger had fallen off the cart during the storm, but both were fine, is what the report said."

"Any word on a dog?"

"No."

"Can I have the names of the medics?"

"Is this on the lottery story? I am surprised no one has called us. Yes, let me give you the name of the driver. He is Chauncey Parsons. He lives in Greenwich. Your best bet is to stop by our offices. Good luck getting anything out of the drivers. They are very discreet."

Becca hung up. She would check out Chauncey later. She now turned attention to another story about a member of parliament with some shady liaisons. Political reporting was her forte. But she loved the offshoot feel good story. She hopped back on the Tube.

The Queen had returned to Buckingham Palace. Her secretary joined her.

"We found the family on the surveillance cameras. But it looks like they paid cash to enter the Castle. SO, we don't have his name. We did not pick up any names on audio surveillance, either. He was always way behind them. Typical, Dad, huh?"

"All right. Go ahead and keep in touch with Becca. And don't involve intelligence. Let's view this more as a fun Treasure hunt."

Becca arrived at the Parliament building. Some members ran for cover. Others were eager to provide information on their adversaries. She took notes, but was lost in thought on the trail to the King. Who was he? Did he really exist?

She again trolled for stories. One caught her eye. She was a big fan of the football league. She loved her London football team. A new player was to be introduced tonight. A free agent. She immediately went online to purchase a ticket. This would be her dime. She was not a beat reporter for the team. She had reported on the team fresh out of college. But she was transferred to the political department, after it was discovered she had been dating one of the star young players. She often thought of him. He had left her. That was a bitter memory.

She left the Parliament to head back to the office. She had a flash back to the weekend. A sixty something couple that had been looking at her. *Winston. Could it be? He was American, judging by the accent. He was at least sixty. No one had mentioned a wife or a daughter. I don't think so. Interesting.*

Becca arrived at her office. She called the hospital back and made up a story about her Aunt. She was connected to a nurse on one of the floors. She chatted about her Aunt. Her Aunt had been in and out of the hospital the last year with complications from diabetes, but the connection was enough to establish the trust for a conversation.

"I hear a King is healing people. Any children suddenly check out of your hospital?" Becca coyly and playfully asked. She was thinking of the smock in the trash can, but wanted to keep it general.

"Odd that you asked. I had not made that connection. People are secretly gossiping about a healing King. One from Atlantis. Once I heard about Atlantis, I turned off the chatter. Nonsense, of course. But we did have four patients leave our hospital. The mothers came by to pick up their belongings. They were all terminally ill. I thought it strange that they all came by at the same time. The mothers had taken their children to Hyde Park for one last day in the sun. All four were going to hospice, today. But yes, they all did leave the hospital. I have not heard anything since. I tried calling, but none of the mothers would talk to me. One said everything was good, and thanked me dearly for all that I done."

"Do you have their names, or towns that they live in?"

"That is private, of course, but why do you care? Oh, I know you, you are the reporter. I could lose my job over this. Let me give you the name of the mother who did talk to me. You need to protect your informant, you know, like all good journalists. Although I don't believe in fairy tales, I would love the story of the King from Atlantis to be true," Nurse Wanda snickered to herself. Later she would tell Nurse Beatrice that the reporters were on the trail.

"You have my word."

Becca's heart was pounding. She took down the name, number and address of the cooperative mother. She took down the private full name, number and address of the nurse. Things were starting to pile drive. Her excitement overwhelmed her, and she leaned back to catch her breath and wipe her brow, even though her office was cool.

Her smartphone buzzed. It was her Aunt. The nurse must have called her. She called her Aunt.

"I had to use you as a connection, and you were there," Becca responded, hearing that the nurse had called her Aunt Grace.

"Becca, my dear niece, that is not why I am calling. The nurse told me about the King from Atlantis on Monday."

"Oh, you want me to find the King to heal you, I see."

"No, Becca."

"What then?"

There was a long silence. Becca leaned forward in her chair.

"I was healed by the King. I have chanted 'Long Live the King!' a hundred times since last Sunday night. I was at the play, Romeo and Juliet, last Sunday night. We all held hands at the end of the play, at the request of the lead actor and actress. There was this enormous energy that transfused through all of us. My diabetes is gone. I feel the best I have felt in years. I look ten or more years younger. Everyone who held hands that night was healed. No one identified the King. But I did see a sixty something year old man sneak backstage at the final intermission. I could see he was talking to the lead actress. I think it was him. He must have told them to call for the union of hands. He was in the front row. He was with a woman, likely his wife, and a younger woman, likely his daughter. He looked American. I say that, because he donned a golf cap when he went outside. I tried to follow him, but he got lost in the crowd. His girls were both blondes and colorfully dressed. Quite pretty, actually, the two of them were. He was handsome, I thought, with a pearly smile, and sky blue eyes. His hair was thin on top. I think he is the King. His ladies didn't seem too aware of his powers. That is just my observation in hindsight," Aunt Grace spoke quickly, the words gushing from her mouth. She had not told anyone her observations, or that she was better. She had told Nurse Wanda, when the nurse told her story. But they made a pact to keep their secrets. She had stayed inside for two days, undecided on what to say about her suddenly youthful looks, and spry mobility.

Again, Becca, was speechless.

"Becca?"

"Aunt Grace, this is momentous. This story is so huge. Can I meet you tomorrow for tea at your home? You can help me here as an investigator. Will you? Maybe the Playhouse would have his name?

"Doubtful. There would be so many names. Too many to isolate him, even if he cooperated. And he may have paid cash."

"It's worth a try. You know, they may be trying to find out, too!"

"See you tomorrow, Sweetie!"

Becca trolled for stories again. Still nothing. She had a flash memory of John Chester Jones. He had changed her life so dramatically. She wondered how he was. She had visited him two years ago at a soldiers' home. He was with his childhood friend, who had gained him admittance to the home, too. He would not talk to her. It was if it was somehow her fault. The pain of betrayal and being dumped returned. But she felt sympathy for him. On top of the world, one moment, and then forgotten and alone. His own parents had given up on him. And she noticed that he had lost his legs. The public only knew he had lost use of his legs, and was in a wheel chair. There was no public sympathy for him, either. He was only as good as his last goal, and given his bad boy character, it was thought of good riddance when he had his fateful wreck.

Becca's smart device buzzed again. "Now what?"

She answered the phone. It was the secretary to the Queen.

"And have you found anything more?" the secretary asked.

"And have you? A trade is only in order, by golly!"

"Becca, we have something, but you first."

"I am following up on the man who won the lottery in Greenwich. Have you heard about him?"

"I heard he won, yes. How does that relate to this?"

"He says he was struck by lightning. But more importantly, he was with another gentleman who was also hit. I think it may be the King."

"Interesting. Well, we had a man at Windsor Castle yesterday asking for a meeting with the Queen, claiming he was the King. The guard escorted him out of the Castle, of course. But the Queen said she had felt a strong presence. We determined that he was with his wife and daughter, but we do not have a name for him. But we do have his image," the secretary eagerly shared her find.

"Well, you are generous with your information. My Aunt called me. She was at the Playhouse the night of the play Romeo and Juliet. As you know there were rumors of chants by patrons of the play of 'Long Live the King!' as they left. My Aunt Grace said they all held hands at the end of the play. She said she has been healed of her diabetes. She thinks everyone at the play was healed of their maladies and ailments. She saw a man in his sixties go backstage at intermission. She suspected he told the actors to ask everyone to hold hands. She suspects he is the King. And, he had a wife and daughter. Were they blondes? Did he have thinning hair?"

"I must meet your Aunt. I will show her the video image. Maybe we are close to finding the King! If we do find him, the Queen requests a meeting with him first, before there is any publicity. Understood?"

"Yes."

"The women were blondes. But the father a full hairline, just shaved close to his skin. Maybe that is the same appearance."

"I am not sure we are close. He is American. He may have already left. But I want to break the story first. Understood?"

"Of course. We need a name. Let's see if the theater will cooperate. He used cash at the Castle, so maybe he used cash at the theater, too."

"British intelligence could find his identity by scanning his image?"

"Possibly, but the Queen is against that now. It is the two of us, I think for now. And Aunt Grace."

"Good-Bye!"

"Good-Bye."

The conversations were always terse and businesslike, with little idle talk. Becca was fired up. The King was real. People were healed. How many others were healed. Many more she speculated. Time to get ready for the game.

10.

BECCA ARRIVED at the sold-out stadium, Wednesday night. The London football team had an important game with the team from Manchester. Both were near the top of the standings. Becca was not dressed as a reporter. She dressed like she had in college. Shorts with a team tee shirt, loosely fitting over her athletic frame. She saw heads swivel as she strutted by with her long legs, and white sneakers. Her hair was down and flowing, held back only by a hair ban, lifting her front hair tall above her hairline. She often was said to look like Princess Grace of so long ago.

She took her seat, only five rows from the field. And near the middle of the field as well. She spared no expense for this one. She was still an avid fan, but had not dated an athlete since Chester. The crowd was abuzz. A new player. A critical game. She was so excited about the game, about the King, about the trust of the Queen in her investigative skills. She was loyal to the core to British royalty. She had never met or spoken to the Queen, but had developed a comfortable relationship with her secretary. Although she did not cover the Crown, the Crown's thoughts on politics and policy were fair game. And she had always protected the Crown, when needed.

She sat next to wealthy men on either side of her. Both were with their spouses, so they only made small talk with her, much to their chagrin. She caught them taking glimpses at her at every chance. But when the players took the field, all eyes were on the game.

She stood and roared with the crowd. She perused the sideline for a glimpse of the new player. She still knew all the players, their names and likeness, position, and statistics. She had an eidetic memory, and steel trap mind. She recalled stats from years past, all the way back to when she was seven years old, the year her father took her to her first game. Her father had passed, but she recalled him with fondness. He was a career diplomat, and she had periodically lived across continents with him and her mother. But he died shortly before she entered Oxford. She now lived with her Mum, next door to her Mum's sister, her Aunt Grace. She had her own space and privacy, when needed. But her Mum was her best friend, and she loved her Aunt Grace dearly. *I am so glad she is better! Oh, the King. I wonder if he likes British "soccer"? Probably, just American football. Probably a Patriots fan. I can't wait to see the video images. A King! From Atlantis! How is that possible? Fun stuff!*

The game started. The crowd roar was deafening. Her part of the stadium never sat down. She sipped her ale with delight. She finished it quickly and wanted another. She did not see a new player. But there were some players sitting on the bench with sweat suits on. One was wearing a hoodie.

The game was nil-nil at halftime. The possession was equal. The passing was deft and accurate. The best players in the world were in the League. Becca enjoyed every pass and every steal. Each side had one shot on net. Both were sure shots, saved beautifully by the goalies.

Becca talked to the gentleman in his fifties next to her on her right side. He had a full head of silvery hair, and wore a blue blazer with a red ascot. He had on khaki pants, and expensive loafers. He certainly was a man of wealth and importance. His wife was dressed in designer jeans, and wore expensive designer shoes. But she had on a team sweatshirt over her silk blouse in support of her team.

"When is the new player to be introduced? I don't see him on the bench," she asked him, her eyes dancing in a flirting way.

"Um. I have not seen him either. The announcers say he is on the bench. He is wearing the hoodie. His name is Jay Jones. They are not sure where he is from. Quite the mystery. They think it is just a marketing ploy," he answered in a serious tone, as his wife observed his response.

"Yes, good idea, to listen to the broadcast team."

The wife gave her the briefest, yet somewhat threatening look. A warning across the bow. Becca left for another ale, and a pretzel.

As she was under the stadium, young men approached her with all the lines she had heard so many times. She finally went to the Ladies toilet for privacy. She checked her smartphone. Oddly, there as a text from her good college friend and fellow football player, Amanda. She had invited her for tea tomorrow afternoon. She wanted to show her a painting. Tomorrow was stacking up to be big day. *And I need to see those images. What if he is Winston?* She would have to prioritize her meetings. Her editor was not interested in the King story. She would have to report a new political story by noon. *Amanda! I have not heard from her in so long! Her hideous scars drove her to the underground, literally, in her basement. My god, you don't suppose she is...*

Becca returned to her seat. She thought of her own secret condition. She was barren, unable to bear children. She had beat ovarian cancer, but the surgery had removed her vital reproductive organs. Maybe that is why she was so interested in the King story. Maybe so. She had not dated anyone since the surgery. Tonight, was her first night she had even dressed in a tempting way. Based on her attention from so many gallant young men, she felt she still was attractive. She still turned heads when dressed professionally. But her attitude must have been intimidating, as few men ever approached her. She thought back to her glamourous glory years before her operation. But then the game began and her fanatic love for her team took over her thoughts.

The crowd roared, and Becca was on her feet. The game continued on with splendid passing and gutsy defense. Each goalie made another spectacular save. As the time wound down, Becca saw the man with hoodie walk towards his coach. It appeared he may go into the game. Becca would not take her eye off of his hoodie. Finally, he took off his sweatshirt and pants, and went to the sideline to enter the game. The crowd roared again.

The gentleman with silvery hair slapped her five. "He is going into the game. He is not a marketing ploy. The announcers are wondering if he is the brother of the former great player, Chester Jones."

Becca stopped breathing. She saw the billowy jet black hair, the broad shoulders, thin waist, and powerful legs. He sure looked like a Jones. It was not Chester of course, as he was incapacitated. She fell back into her seat, as the crowd roar was deafening when Jay Jones entered the game.

She finally stood, and watched the action. Jay Jones was dribbling the ball near her sideline. She saw his face. She flushed crimson red and hyperventilated. If Jay was his brother, he was an identical twin!

Then, it was like magic. Jay Jones broke free with the ball. He sprinted towards the goal with one defender to beat. The defender went to tackle him, but Jay deftly cut around him. The goalie charged out to block the angle. Jones struck too quickly. The ball sailed into the net. The crowd erupted into its loudest cheer of the night. Becca's ears were ringing from the thunderous, raucous roar.

And then the murmur started. It started in the seats behind the goal, and slowly moved around the stadium.

Becca was trembling. The gentleman with silvery hair asked if she was all right. He took off his blazer and put it over her shoulders. His wife approved, witnessing the wretched shape Becca appeared to be in.

"We love you Chester! And if it's quite all right, we love you Chester!'

The gentleman with silvery hair says to her, "the crowd thinks it is John Chester Jones! The broadcasters say it may be a miracle. But maybe Chester had been working all these years to regain feeling and motion in his legs. They are flabbergasted. Maybe Jay is a twin they are saying. What is going on!"

Becca was so stunned. She knew it was Chester. He was her first true love after college. She had broken off her relationship with her college boyfriend, who had gone to New York City to work on Wall Street for a preeminent investment bank.

"He did not have legs," she said quietly, not so sure it was him anymore. *But the King could have given him his legs!*

"What?" the husband and wife said.

"Long Live the King!!" Becca shouted at the top of her lungs. Energy burst through from her deepest self, and emboldened her to work even harder on her story.

"Long Live the King!" She shouted again.

Soon others joined the chant. The chant started to rival the Chester tribute.

Jay Jones heard the chant. He was stunned that the crowd would know. He suspected most thought he had rehabilitated, as the public did not know his legs had been lost. But still, he had kept the encounter with the King a secret. He raised his hand to air, as if acknowledging the crowd.

The crowd was in a frenzy. It did not know what to believe or expect. The game ended. The crowd would not leave. Becca slipped away, out of the stadium. Another visit tomorrow. The soldier's home.

11.

BECCA PREPARED FOR her busy day, that Thursday. She made out a calendar of events.

The list began. Breakfast with Aunt Grace. Tea with Amanda. A visit to the soldier's home. A visit to the cooperating mother. A visit to the medical emergency office in Greenwich. A visit to Buckingham Palace. A long day.

But her mind could not let go of the image of Jay Jones. The media was abuzz on who he was. He had not done any interviews. Team management was silent. The cognoscenti claimed it was John Chester Jones. His parents had once called him Jay. He did not have a twin brother. He must have rehabilitated his legs in private institutions that had been very discreet.

Becca thought and knew differently. She did not recall any twin brother, she was sure of that. A lost twin brother like in the movie Parent Trap was not in the cards. His parents were divorced, but not until he was in high school. It was doubtful a twin was put up for adoption, even though his parents were impecunious when he was born. Some in the media speculated that was the case. One headline even said it was a classic story of the prodigal lost son.

But Becca had seen John Chester Jones with no legs. She had seen him put on his prosthetic limbs. She had seen his frustration, and his anger. So, she decided it was either a twin brother, which she deduced was highly unlikely, or John Chester Jones had been healed by the King. She was determined to prove the latter. Oddly, the media was silent on the King, as it had been from the beginning. As far as she knew, she was the only one gathering intelligence on the King.

Becca headed to see her Aunt first. She gathered details of the play. She did not gather much more intelligence than Aunt Grace had told her over the phone. But Aunt Grace looked magnificent. She then headed to Mayfair. She rang the doorbell. She was greeted by a little boy.

"Hi, are you here to see Amanda? Are you Miss Hollingsworth! Please, come in. She is expecting you," Mark Buckingham announced proudly, wearing brand new clothes bought for him by Amanda earlier in the week. His dark brown hair had grown thick and velvety since Sunday.

"You are quite handsome! Thank you, young sir for your welcome!"

"Follow me."

Mark took Becca by the hand. She felt the remnants of the energy force tingle her hand and fingers. Chills went up her spine. Down a staircase, through a door, and down another spiral staircase to the basement they traveled. There, they walked into Amanda's hideout from society, that now was her magnificent studio come to life.

Amanda had her back to Becca. Her flowing auburn hair was thick and resilient. It flowed in the breeze from a near-by fan.

"Hello, my dear friend. You must be on the trail of this story, I am sure!" Amanda coyly said, her voice playful and firm.

Becca's chills continued to shiver all over her body. She walked closer to Amanda, her best friend at Oxford. She had tried to keep in close contact with Amanda, but Amanda had shut her out of her life, not completely, but only barely connected through occasional social media forays. She had seen her terrible scars and marks from the fire. But she saw through them to the kind little rich girl, who carried no airs about her, even with her parent's enormous wealth. Amanda always said that all the Kings men and all the Kings horses could not put Humpty Dumpty back together again. The Kings of course were the best doctors in the United Kingdom. After years of failures, she receded into a reclusive purgatory, so most thought. But Amanda had left her home often, covering her face with her scarf. And she sought to help others less fortunate than her. She was already serving the common good.

And now it was a real King who may have saved her and healed her.

Becca looked at the priceless painting of the Princess, that Amanda has saved the night of the fire. It was still stunning and moving. But her eye then moved to a new painting. She stared at the new painting. It was illuminating and brilliant. It was a Palace of inordinate beauty and architectural brilliance. It looked like a Palace from another time, or even another planet or universe. *Atlantis.* That is what Becca could see, for sure, she thought. Behind the Palace appeared to be a Temple, and a backdrop of a bay, with bright blue water, and twelve monument-like pillars, all rock formations, in the ocean on the other side of the land barrier forming the bay, underneath a blue sky with lazy puffy white clouds floating above the pillars, that completed the painting.

And then the moment of truth. Amanda turned and gazed at her loyal friend. Becca fell backwards in awe and shock. Mark caught her and moved her to a comfortable chair. She was breathless again.

"The King?"

"I knew you would be on this story. We who have been healed have kept our silence. But observers and passersby have spread rumors. I am surprised the media has not jumped on this."

"It is such fancy and such a fairy tale. No one believes any more in fantasy, or magic, or miracles. Only in video games, and then, those games are mostly about war. But I believe. My Aunt was at the play at the Playhouse. So many were healed at that play. Soon, with six degrees of separation, the number of people in contact with healed people will be large. The secret will be told. Whether it is believed, I don't know."

"Becca, you have always been one to love the dream, the fantastic, the boundless, the imagination, the splendor of life, and the expansive scientific, mathematical possibilities of our universe and beyond. I am surprised you report on politics, why not science?"

"Politics sells papers and our website. Yes, I love the intersection of science, and fantasy. Yesterday's fantasy is today's science. But Amanda, you are so beautiful. More so, than even before. What was it like to be healed? Did you see bright white light? Did you see this Palace and Temple from Atlantis? Did you see God? Tell me more. And who is this King? I have gathered he is an American, with a wife and a daughter. But I don't know much more. But he did try to meet the Queen!"

"I did not see bright lights or lightning! Yes, I believe the maintenance worker must have been with the King! But I felt tremendous energy flow through me. I saw white energy around my limbs. I did not see Atlantis, until some dreams that Sunday night. I immediately tasked myself to paint the Palace and the Temple. I believe the King was once the King of Atlantis in a past life. I saw it in his eyes.

They carried centuries of time. He looked so regal, and so wise. Monday night I dreamt of the end of Atlantis. Oceans swallowed it up! So many perished. I may paint that as a second painting. The King told me to focus on my paintings. I have."

"What did he say to you?"

"I am the once and former King of Atlantis. Upon my word, you shall be healed. So, it shall be said, so, it shall be done. You are hereby healed. Go, and serve the common good."

Becca sat back and reflected.

And then you said, "Long Live the King!"

"Yes, we did, the young boy added with emotion. He repeated the chant three times, before Amanda held her index to her lips.

"And who are you, young gentleman?"

"I am Mark Buckingham! I was a terminally ill orphan who had escaped from the hospice, a flat in the Southwark Borough. I was at the right time and place, I suppose. I remember you in a dream that Saturday night, too."

He dropped his eyes, knowing his good fortune.

"A couple of young men were sneering at my looks last Saturday afternoon, and Mark came over afterwards and said I was pretty. He brought me a flower. I gave it to a blind man, one who I brought cookies to, from time to time. He, of course, could not see my hideous looks."

"Mark and I had visions that Saturday night of healing. I think the King visited me in my dreams. The next day, the King approached us, Mark, me, the blind man, who had been healed the night before, and his ailing mother. He healed all three of us. The blind man left. I have not heard from him. I think he had a long-lost love, who he may have abandoned, or shut out of his life, like I did, to so many friends and family. It was a miracle, for sure. His mother danced away in song. He cried for joy. Mark may be become my foster brother. I will know tonight. Mum and Dad return from India. I will let you know."

"Do they know about you?"

"No, they don't. I am not sure what they will do. Of course, they will say it is modern medicine. They will not believe in the King."

"Becca, do you know his name. I would like to thank him some time from now. His spirit will last beyond this lifetime, but he certainly, won't. I did not know he had a wife and daughter. I fancied being his Queen a few times! Ha!"

"Yes, he was at Windsor Castle with his wife and daughter. At least, the man we thing may be the King, was there. I will see pictures of him tonight from video surveillance at the Castle. And the man who saved the jumper at the Tower Bridge was said to be accompanied by a sixty-year-old man, too."

"The maintenance worker said his fellow lightning victim was a sixty-year-old man, too!"

"I did not see that. But the healings were before the lightning strike, so lightning must not be the cause of the King's magnificent power."

"I will show you a photo of the video images. If you confirm his likeness, we know it is him!"

"Indeed. I would love to help."

Becca hugged Amanda for a long time. She was getting closer.

"Did you see the game on television last night?" Amanda asked.

Becca stopped in her tracks. She sat down on a couch. Amanda walked over and sat next to her. Mark sensed a frost in the air.

"You know, Becca, it was never my intention."

"Did you ever go out with him?"

"I did not. I told him to stay away from me. He said he always wanted to go out with me, that he was intimidated by me, and that he went out with you to get to know me. I told him that was beyond reproach to use my best friend that way. I told him that he broke your heart. He was persistent. But he showed his true colors. Once the fire occurred, he stopped calling, stop courting, stopped everything.

"At first, he tried to seduce me here at the house, when I was with another boy, and you were here. I slapped him, of course. And said I would never date a boyfriend of my best friend. That is when he decided to break up with you. He tried to seduce me again the next week. I told him that was not my intention in telling him I would not date him while he dated you! He was persistent all the way until the fire. Sorry Becca."

Becca stared at the painting while Amanda spoke.

"I thought that was the case. He complained to me about you. He had the audacity to ask me to help him win your affection. I am certain that was him, last night. But only if the King worked his magic."

"What do you mean? The commentators thought he may have rehabilitated his legs."

"I saw him a year ago. He had no legs!"

"So, Jay Jones is a twin, or the King healed him. Becca, it must have been the Atlantean King. The two men who heckled me, when Mark gave me the flower were in wheel chairs, and without legs. I thought I knew one of them, but I could not place him. My memory is more vivid now. It was John Chester Jones. I did not know the other fellow."

"That makes so much sense. This story grows by leaps and bounds every day. His friend was a James Tudor. He was a soldier in the foreign wars. He was a childhood friend of Chester. I had met him at the soldier's home when Chester and I were together. Chester visited him once every Sunday. He was a loyal friend. I wonder if James has been healed, too."

"I am sure he has," Mark attested, brushing back his black locks flopping on his forehead.

"You have quite the new mane of hair, Mark Buckingham!" teased Amanda.

"Becca, I still don't think you are over him. I never liked him, at least not as a boyfriend. I will make that clear if he ever courts me again."

"He will no longer be the bad boy. He will serve the common good. I believe he will be a nice person, like he was with his friend," Mark chimed in again, proud of his insight.

Becca looked solemn.

"Becca, I know your situation. We need to find the King for you. We will get him back to London. Maybe we can find his daughter. I bet she lives in Southwark," Amanda said, putting her arm around the slumping Becca.

"That would be nice. Last night I dressed down a bit. The boys were all over me! I may still have it. But, who would marry me now. I need to see the King."

"Not to be chirping, but there are a lot of kids out there that would love to have you as a foster Mum," Mark told her, a little mist in his eyes.

Becca sat back and reflected on that comment.

"Yes, that is a solution. I can still get married, to the right understanding guy. But, I still would like my own children. I want to see the King."

Becca stood and hugged Amanda again. She kissed Mark on the forehead.

"Good luck with Amanda's parents tonight. If it doesn't work, I am sure my Aunt Grace will take you in as a foster child," Becca assured him, a tear in her eye now, too.

"Wait, he is my little brother!" laughed Amanda.

"Always competing for the attention of the most eligible bachelors!" Becca winked.

Mark laughed, and went upstairs to play some video games. Becca left for her next meeting.

In an hour, after a few rides and changeovers on the Tube, Becca arrived at the soldier's home. There was an architect taking measurements. She found the head administrator in her office.

"I am here to see James Tudor."

"They told me you might come."

Becca looked puzzled at first, but then expected the reason.

"They both left, didn't they? Both well, I presume."

"They did not leave. They just never came back. Then on Tuesday, we received a check from a trust for one million pounds, for renovations, and high tech gadgetry. It was anonymous, but I suspect it was from Jay Jones. Yes, I know that was Chester on television last night. I know his eyes better than anyone. Except, maybe you! He lost all of his money from gambling, his high lifestyle, and then litigation and medical expenses. But his parents had died, and left him money in trust. He had told me about that. He loved this home so much. We took good care of him. Of course, he was not a soldier, but we let him here anyway. All of the other soldiers loved him, the former great playboy, bad boy, awesome football player. He said if he ever was healed, he would pay us back. I guess he did," the administrator just stared at her.

"Have you seen James?"

"No, but he had a long-lost love interest, maybe was even his wife once. She wrote him weekly, and he had never returned her letters. That is so old fashioned, writing letters, not emails or social media. He read them all though. She lived in Edinburg, in Scotland. I suppose that is where he is. I am happy for him. I am sure she took him back in open arms. She used to visit, but he would not see her. She just wrote after that. There is not much more I can tell you."

"How do you think they were healed?"

"I think you know. Long Live the King!"

"Long Live the King!"

With that Becca left. She hugged the administrator, a lady in her late fifties. Back to the tube she went, on her way to Kensington.

12.

ECCA ARRIVED at the stately home in Kensington of Stuart and Merle Smith, and their daughter Shaylee, very late that afternoon. The heavy wooden door of the three-story brownstone had a brass knocker in the shape of a gargoyle. She saw expensive drapes hiding behind the long windows on either side of her. A beautiful and manicured garden with abundant autumn flowers cheered up her spirit. She had called Mrs. Smith, who agreed to talk to her. Her husband was on a business trip in Hong Kong. He was head of international sales for a large pharmaceutical company.

Mrs. Smith answered the door, and invited Becca inside for tea. Becca sat down in a formal chair with a high back, and a flowered fabric. Mrs. Smith sat across from her. Mrs. Smith opened the conversation. She went right to the point.

"Shaylee is back at school, for the first time this fall. She had made it through last school year, before lapsing back into what became a final terminal affliction of her cancer-a rare blood cancer. She was on her final days, about to enter hospice. Three other kids were similarly situated. The three mothers and I decided to take them one last time to the park for a picnic, before they entered hospice. Their spirits were high that day. I don't know if they anticipated the arrival of the King from Atlantis, or not. But a sense of calm and even frivolity seemed to fill the air."

"Where were the husbands?"

"They were all working, preparing to take time off for the final few days. Stuart was in town. He eventually met us at the London Eye. As a family, we stayed on it for another hour. Even Stuart was chanting 'Long Live the King!'"

"Why have not people gone to the press about this?"

"I don't know. Shaylee told us not to go to the press. I asked her why? She said that is what the King wanted. But she offered no explanation, and said she only felt that, he did not order her to keep silent. I gather that must be the case. No healed people have come forth. Other than the lottery winner! And he is giving credit to the lightning!"

"I think that is a common pattern. Rumors fly. And those rumors are by spectators and bystanders. But they have no corroboration. And family members are sticking to the silent strategy. But I have found out a lot. It is not that I want to blow the cover off the story. But I want to find out what I can. I want to meet this man. This man who would be or was a King," Becca stated professionally.

"I suspect there is more, Becca. You want to be healed. I know you were out for a while. I am an avid reader of your reported stories and your weekly editorial. I saw him. He is an American, maybe sixty or so years old. He had the bluest eyes, and wore a golf cap. He had a beaming smile, with straight and white teeth. I heard his laugh. It was infectious. He was maybe under six feet tall. But he disappeared after the girls were healed. Do you know what he told them as he held their hands?"

"I have heard from my friend Amanda. But tell me."

"I am the once and former King of Atlantis. Upon my word, you shall be healed. So, it shall be said, so, it shall be

done. You are hereby healed. Go, and serve the common good."

"Yes, that is the same prayer or vigil. And the description fits him. Well, I will keep you posted. And the other Mums?"

"I have called them. They are so happy. Two live away in the countryside a few hours north of the city, and the third is a wife of a fishing boat captain on the southern coast. We plan to get together in the spring in the park! I have their names?"

"Thankyou. I will let them have their privacy. I will only contact them as needed."

"And he healed the two attending nurses, Beatrice and Wanda. We thought of them as angels, even before the real angel came."

"I see."

With that Becca finished her tea, and said good-bye. *Off to Greenwich!*

Becca arrived at the emergency services office. She wanted to meet with the medic who saved the lightning victims. He was there.

"Hi, Miss Hollingsworth. It is a pleasure to meet you. I know you may have heard this. But I do say, you looked outstanding last night on television. They showed you rooting hard on repeated occasions. You did look a little flushed when Jay Jones came into the game, and when he scored. The announcer said you and he were once an item! They used your reaction as a plus factor in whether Jay is Chester Jones or his twin brother," Chauncey Parsons chuckled, while blushing a tad, even though he was rugged and had a deep husky voice.

"And today you look quite professional! You do know that most of the city's bachelors have big crushes on you. In fact, because of you, we are quite up on our political discourse, because we read your reports and editorials!"

Becca was taken aback by his charm and flirtations. But ultimately, she liked and accepted the compliments. But she was floored that she was a spectacle on national television, particularly with her hair down, and college girl attire. But there was no rebuke, or response of any kind from her employer, or family, or coworkers. Not yet anyway. But then again, she had taken herself off of social media on a personal level. And very few had her text and email contacts. But still.

"Mr. Parsons, you are kind in your compliments! But I am here on business! I am not sure that was me on television. Maybe a younger sister!"

"Just trying, that's all. But I would be glad to help you. Let's go to the scene. Shall we? Well, the commentators sure thought that was you!"

"Let's go."

Chauncey took one of the office cars up to the park in Greenwich. They disembarked from the car. Chauncey talked about the game the whole ride over. His take was that Jay Jones was a long-lost twin brother. He said a recent poll on the lead radio station had the twin brother explanation at 55-45 in voting. Becca laughed. She said she was not taking sides.

They walked up the hill towards the Prime Meridian. There to their right was a giant oak tree, split down the middle. The overturned maintenance vehicle had been moved out of the way, but in sight to the right of the tree. Chauncey took her by the hand, and brought her to the tree. A bit away, another tree had fallen, too.

"As you can see, the tree was struck in direct hit. It feels like the tree is still smarting from the blow. We, well, the park service, will remove the tree tomorrow. So, it is good you saw the tree today. Now look at the maintenance vehicle. It is charred. I don't know how there were any survivors. The lottery winner, a fellow of the name Houston Garrison, claims that there were three passengers in the vehicle when the lightning hit, a father, a mother and a daughter. He told me that at the scene, but did not tell the press after he won the lottery. When we arrived, it was only the worker and an elderly man-maybe sixty. They both appeared fine. But I honestly don't know how they survived. I never found the older man after that. We decided to look for him, sensing he could collapse and die. But there were no reports of such an occurrence in any of the hospitals. I presume he survived. We did not find the mother or daughter either, and there were no reports of their demise," Chauncey finished. Becca had pulled away from his grasp of her hand after they had left the tree.

"This is a place of miracles!"

"Wait. There is more. A woman came by the office the next day. She asked about the sixty-year old man. She had seen him in the ship museum with his wife and daughter. She claims that her dog, Jackson, had three legs. But after the lightning struck, it had its fourth leg back, fully healed and active. So, she thought. But her daughter says the dog was running around before the lightning struck. And the daughter saw the sixty something year old man, holding his paws," Chauncey held that statement, waiting for a reaction.

Becca just stared.

"Another miracle. I think it was a miracle the four of them lived. I think it was the old man. And I think it somehow ties into man who was saved at Tower Bridge. And the rumors about the Playhouse."

"And Long Live the King!"

"Yes! Long Live the King!"

"It will be hard to piece this all together in a cohesive, evidence backed story. But yes, the pieces are adding up to a story about a King. Have any other reporters been by?"

"No. A few have met with the lottery winner. But, no one met with us. I think the press views him as nutcase. That he was just lucky, and that he was not even hit by lightning. But I just showed you the proof," Chauncey shrugged his shoulders as he opened his hands, palms up to the sky.

Chauncey looked to the ground.

"I was supposed to keep this quiet. My coworker was seriously burned in a fire on a rescue mission a while back. He lost his hearing, too, in one ear. After the rescue attempt at Greenwich park, well, he recovered his hearing, and his burn injuries are gone. Sure, let's blame the lightning on that, too. But, he told me it was the old man. He was a King. A King in Atlantis! But this is a deep secret. He does not want it told. His name is Pete Copperfield. He has a wife and family. So, yeah, the King is real. Long Live the King!"

"I will keep the secret. At least for now. Well, thank you so much. I think I will walk around and then take the Tube home. If I write a story, I will list you as a credit!"

"Why thank you. If you ever are around here, call me. I can give you a private tour! And by the way, my aching back no longer aches. I am sure that is a coincidence."

"I am sure!"

With that, Becca left.

On her way down, a text file came in. She opened quickly. It was a picture of the man who said that he was the King at Windsor Castle.

She dropped to her knees, and then half crawled to a park bench.

"Winston!"

She fired a text back to the secretary.

"His name is Winston!"

A text was fired back.

"Surely, you gest! The reincarnation of our own Winston Churchill, you dare say?"

"No, but that is the name his wife called him."

"Let us meet tomorrow, instead of tonight. We will run the name Winston at the airport. Oh yes, Mi-6 is assisting us now, without the knowledge of the government. A charitable venture, one of national interest, not national security. Bye!"

"Bye!"

Becca started to cry uncontrollably. She was so happy for all of those that were healed. She was happy she was putting together a story, if not a tale, for the ages. But she wanted to be healed, too. And yes, she wanted to see Chester again. She called him Jay. Never Chester. He named himself Jay for the roster. Surely, that was a message for her.

A woman had stood nearby and watched her cry, and eventually stop. The woman was with a dog. She took a seat next to Becca.

"I am a big fan of yours. I heard from Chauncey, that you are investigating the healing King angle to the lightning story," the woman said in a kind voice.

"I don't suppose that dog once had three legs!"

"You are jolly right! Of course, Chauncey told you about the dog. I come here every day, hoping to see the man. The King! I want to thank him. My daughter has been wonderful since that day. She had suffered from bulimia and depression. She is eating normally, fully stable, and oh so happy. So, is Jackson."

"Tell me more!"

"I saw Jackson running at full tilt. I now recall it was before the lightning. I did not see the family, or the sixty-year-old man. My daughter says he held the dog's paws, then the dog ran. Some kind of miracle. A regeneration. I have no clue how it is possible. Especially, as it was instantaneous. Maybe some kind of huge energy field, and a time-space continuum, where time veered off for a moment, while the hind leg regenerated. I don't know. I read a lot. But I still feel residual energy. It has even rubbed off on me. I usually have migraine headaches. I have not had one since the lightning storm. Hold the dog's paws."

Becca held Jackson's paws. She felt some tingling, and even saw some residual light. She was not certain, and knew the power of suggestion was strong.

"Maybe. Maybe. This is such an incredible story. Certainly, if it is true, the floodgates may open for Winston. Maybe he could scientifically determine how he is doing the healing, and give the gift of healing to science and mankind. But I suspect he does not know. He claims to have been a former King of Atlantis. If that is true, and Atlantis was a beacon of technology beyond what we know today, and if he truly is a reincarnation of his former regal soul, and if his memory his cross temporal and spatial, or if he pulls energy from the past space-time location, through some type of wormhole, or portal through time and space, and utilizes that energy to heal, and on and on I can go, maybe he can pass on this power to mankind!"

"Atlantis! Winston! Was he also Winston Churchill?"

"Oh, I don't believe so. We think that may be his present name. And yes, in his incantation prior to each healing, he stated he was the former King of Atlantis."

"That is so much to follow and understand. I will just believe, because I have physical and visual proof in the here and now of the healing that occurred. Whether it was King Winston, or the lightning, I don't care. But the fancy and wonder of a healing King is so fun to believe!"

"You probably heard there are other stories of healing?"

"Sort of, but only rumblings and musings. Someone mentioned a mass healing at the Playhouse. That would be nice if more were healed."

"Well, I am getting to the bottom of this, and I hope to meet the King someday. I wonder what his name was in Atlantis. Surely, not Winston. I am off. I am tired. I am going home. What a day! Thank you so much for telling me your story. If I do publish a story, may I include your story? And what is your name? And did you catch the names of his wife and daughter?"

"I am Johanna Stark. I am thirty-eight. My daughter is Savannah Stark. She is twelve. I am a widow. Yes, we would love to be part of your story! No, we did not catch their names."

Johanna brushed back her brown hair, and smiled broadly. A few tears trickled down her pink cheeks, flushed with excitement, as she watched one of London's finest walk away.

Becca arrived at her apartment in Chelsea. She made herself some melba toast with guacamole and salmon on top. She sipped down a glass of rose, and passed out in exhaustion on her couch.

13.

WINSTON SIPPED his Starbucks coffee, and ate his Starbucks spinach feta breakfast sandwich, while he read an article on the benefits of probiotics. He determined he would eat more yogurt, sauerkraut and pickles, starting the next day.

He was back in Westminster, in his sunroom in the back of his very New England colonial home. It was Saturday, a week since that first fateful day. Every day since his return from London, he thought of the odyssey of his healing journey. He had not entered the realm, or time-space continuum, or other energy field, or whatever place or state of being it was, that he had entered into in London.

Maybe it was London. Maybe London was originally part of the empire of Atlantis. Maybe the energy was there, in London, for him to draw upon, as a former Supreme Priest, and former King of Atlantis.

But he was sure that it had happened. He himself felt the best he had in years. He had been healed in the lightning storm. Mary had secretly gone to her heart doctor for testing. She could not hold the secret for long. She told Winston she was healed. She asked him if he had anything to do with it. She often thought Winston was aloof and out there, but now believed he truly was out there, in another realm. He said nothing, just that he felt better, too. And Elizabeth had called to say her knee and back were better. That rumors were floating around in London about people being healed at the Playhouse, and that they were there! So, the rumors were likely true, and the Playhouse was the source of her feeling better. Unlike Mary, Elizabeth did not suspect her father was the man behind the miracles. Today, Winston, said, he would try to harness his powers again. Then he would know if London was the sole source of his powers.

Winston went to his country club. One of the members had suffered a stroke. He had overcome tremendous obstacles and hurdles to return to the golf course, but still suffered from setbacks from the stroke, including no use of his lower left leg. He was very close friend of Winston.

Winston met him at the club. He told him the stories in London. His friend was crying the whole time.

"We all knew you were special. Even an angel. And now it is true. I don't believe in Atlantis, but I do believe in angels and miracles!" His friend stated. He combed back his impeccably groomed white hair, and brushed his white goatee with his fingers.

"I will go to London, if that is the source of your power. But try it here first!"

"Maybe Connecticut was once part of Atlantis, too. Or a colony of Atlantis. Maybe the Atlanteans took their power crystals here, and they are buried under rock and sediment. It was the power crystals, I believe, that powered their communications, transportation, energy, and even healing, when channeled by priests and holy men. There was some type of connection to other realms of existence, whether spiritual, or different dimensions in time and space, or even parallel universes or worlds. Somehow, I can access that energy now. I am not sure how. But it is likely because I had achieved such a high status in Atlantean society, as both the Supreme Priest, and then the King. Somehow, I have been able to connect back to my past, and bring the energy forth. But it is not volitional. It just sort of happens. But at the end, it seemed to be more in my control. I could see auras of people. And when someone was in need, the energy would flow."

Winston called his friend Saint Nick, as he looked like Santa Claus.

"Saint Nick, you need to keep this as our secret. I have not told anyone about this, not even Mary," Winston said, relieved he had finally told someone, but apprehensive, that the old rumor mill would now roll, as the person, Saint Nick, would tell just one person, probably his wife, or his golf partner, and tell them not to tell anyone else, but that one person would tell just one person, and so on. Soon the avalanche of the single rumor would spread through an intricate tapestry of communication lines. But it would not be publicly discussed, as everyone kept it secret, until at a party, one person would overhear the rumor, confirm he had heard the rumor, too, and the whole party would then discuss the rumor publicly, and the rumor would be confirmed as a fact.

Winston wondered if, or when the rumor, went public, and was confirmed, as true, how his life would be transformed. It might be local, where individuals would ask to be healed in a genteel fashion. Or there might be a stampede! Or the media might get ahold of the rumor, and lambast him as a fraud, or hold him up as a hero, or angel, or alien, or even, what he thought of as the truth, the reincarnation of an Atlantean King, which would draw more skepticism, or awe, or cynicism, or glory, or even a coronation. Athletes and aging actors would want to hire him for pay, governments would want to regulate his activities. On and on,

Winston thought. His former legal mind raced to see all the angles, all the solutions, all the pitfalls, all the potential problems, all the potential profits. But all he wanted was his simple, now retired life, and to heal people on the fly, underground, and out of the public eye.

Winston grabbed Saint Nick. "Don't tell anyone, not your spouse, or any of the guys. You know, you tell one person, and tell them to keep it a secret, and they tell just one person and tell them to keep it a secret, and soon everyone knows."

"I understand, soon anytime anyone has a cold they will want you to heal them. Or the whole world will camp out in Westminster and line up to see you. I get it. But what do I say, when I am healed!"

"You are already the living embodiment of a miracle! It is not far-fetched that you will be totally healed from your rehabilitation. And all of your arthritis will be gone, too. And of course, I will heal King Richard of all of his ailments, too, and Donny boy of his back problems. But it will be in time, and under the umbrage of friendship and trust," Winston gained strength with his words, and trust in his friend.

"Let us go to the river. Water is the key to all life. Water is connected throughout the world. The river is connected to the Atlantic Ocean, which is connected to the Thames River. So, maybe I can draw energy anywhere in the world if I am near a waterway that is connected to the oceans."

Saint Nick grabbed his cane. As he did, as if they were eavesdropping, or connected in mind, King Richard and Donny Boy, both nicknames, too, arrived.

Saint Nick called to them.

"We are going to the river for a swim. Come on, boys."

The two of them laughed. But they saw the seriousness of their two friends, particularly, Winston Churchill.

Sir Richard was a retired salesman in the financial services industry. He was a legendary runner with broad shoulders who had fallen on hard times, having beaten cancer, pancreatitis, blood issues and more, but still suffered from complications from all of them. Donny boy was a retired communications executive who had a reconstructed back, that hobbled him, and caused him great pain and suffering. Saint Nick was a retired medical products entrepreneur. All had time and money, but did not have the health to enjoy it. Sir Richard had short gray hair, and Donny Boy, who had shrunk four inches from his raging back, had silvery hair.

Off to a tributary off of the Connecticut River they went. The men were silent. Saint Nick was sworn to secrecy, and feared reprisal if he broke his vow. The other two felt the energy in the Ford F-150 driven by Saint Nick. They also always thought Winston was an angel or special being.

Soon they arrived at a gravelly road that took them to the river bank, where the river took a bend, and the current was slow and the water not deep.

"I am here to heal you. Let's wade into the river. Don't ask questions. This may not work, but I feel the energy welling up inside me. Follow me."

Soon the four men were waist deep in the river. Winston felt the enormous surge of energy. He approached his friends.

"I am the once and former King of Atlantis. Upon my word, you shall be healed. So, it shall be said, so, it shall be done. You are hereby healed. Go, and serve the common good."

All felt the surge of energy, and all saw glimpses of Atlantis. Joy surrounded them. They hooted and hollered like fraternity brothers on a big college weekend.

Winston told Sir Richard and Donny Boy his story. They all would keep it a secret. At least for now.

Saint Nick took them back to the club. They played eighteen holes. All but Winston recorded their lowest rounds in years.

Winston said goodbye.

"I need to return to London."

Winston went home and told Mary his story.

"I have suspected this for years, you know. You should tell Elizabeth and Anne, too."

"I will meet with Anne tomorrow. And I want to fly back to London. I want to find out where the energy source is. It is somewhere in London. There is nothing in the media or the press about the healing or the miracles. The only story I could find is of the maintenance worker who was struck by lightning in the cart with us. He won the lottery the next day!"

"I am fine with that plan. How long will you be?"

"A couple of weeks."

"I will join you if you stay longer than two weeks, or if you summon me earlier. Should I say anything to their wives. Surely, they will know their husbands are miraculously better!"

"No, not now. All of them will attribute it to rehabilitation," Winston said, without conviction, as he wringed his hands, and gazed out the back window at the wooded backyard.

"All right. That is the plan."

14.

ECCA MARCHED into the office of the secretary to the Queen. It was now Monday morning. Her meeting with the secretary had been postponed until Monday.

"I am here. I defer to you, Madam Secretary!"

"Well, we have not found anyone using the name Winston. There were no Americans with the name Winston who left England last Tuesday. And there were no arrivals for the last week. It is possible that is a nickname?"

"A dead end?"

"Well, not necessarily. The Queen's cousin, a second cousin, met with her today to announce his engagement to an elderly widow, and heiress to a shipping fortune. He told her how a man had healed her of Alzheimer's. A man at our most famous department store in his sixties. So, maybe it was this man named Winston! But we are not pursuing the name any further for now, as we have exhausted the search avenues available to us. I am sure you, like me, have searched local and social media and the web for his name."

The secretary continued in a stately manner. "His facial recognition did not turn up either. He may not have been scanned yet in the United Kingdom. We have not been given authority to review the surveillance cameras at the airports to see what flight he and his wife may have boarded. So, we are at ground zero. Except, we do have some guards looking for his daughter in Central London. We suspect she lives in London, based on conversations the guards over-heard. We don't know where she lives, but because so many healings occurred in Central London, we are starting there. They have a video image of her. We don't want to scare her, and have no rights to apprehend her, as she and her father are innocent of any wrongdoing. She may not even know about her father. But if we find her, maybe we can arrange for you to meet her. You are about her age. And even re-semble each other somewhat! She probably knows of you, too."

"I will do that. And maybe he will come back to London to see his daughter."

"That is our best bet. That may be a year, or maybe over the holidays. Or there will be more healings. If so, we can track them quickly."

"Maybe I should do a teaser piece. A short article that maybe he would find and understand, one that would not invite public attention or speculation?"

"Such as?"

"Let me think about that. I have some more people to see and interview. I have more and more leads on people who were at the play on Sunday night. And, well, I think, and I might."

"See Jay Jones?"

"Yes! Have you heard anything?"

"No, we are perplexed and confused like most fans. I suspect, like you, he was healed by the King. And you?"

Becca proceeded to tell the secretary all that she had found out. Amanda had also confirmed the image was the King. The secretary was gracious. Becca looked at her per-fectly set silver hair, and impeccable suit. The secretary was over sixty, but an absolutely brilliant woman, educated at the finest academic institutions in England. The secretary peered over her glasses.

"I have an idea."

Becca stared back, hopeful of a stupendous idea.

"We will have a gala event at the Kensington Palace. We will combine it with the event for the engagement of her cousin. We will invite those that were healed, that we know of, in person. You will invite the King, in some secretive, hidden way. Use that as your teaser piece. I will leave that up to you. But give me the names of all of those that you know of that have been healed."

"Splendid idea! I am so excited. Am I invited, too!"

"I know your ulterior plans!"

"I know. To be healed by the King."

"And?"

"And to meet Chester again. Maybe it is not meant to be, but at least I would know. And there is the blind man. I have not found him. Or the man at the river who saved the Tower Bridge jumper. I have work to do!"

15.

BECCA VENTURED down to London Bridge late that Monday morning. She was going to stay there until she saw the man that saved the London Bridge jumper. She had read that the jumper had filed for bankruptcy, and had hit rock bottom and financial ruin in his life. But after he have been saved, he had reunited with his wife and children. She had, unknown to him, done exceedingly well with her investments with the substantial monetary settlement she had received in the divorce. They paid off all of his creditors. She insisted on a prenuptial agreement, but marital bliss and life happiness had returned. He was starting a charitable foundation, and had created a charitable advisory service for people in financially strapped lives. He was serving the common good.

Becca was cheerful. She was not sure why. Neither the King nor Jay Jones were in her life, at the moment. But the day was sunny, and she had a hunch she might just meet the savior. Or even Winston's daughter. She wore an old Winston red tee shirt that she had found online. It was a promotional shirt for the cigarette brand. Maybe the secret riddle would not have to be solved.

She walked up and down the Riverwalk. She surmised Elizabeth must work, so her efforts there were likely fruitless until the evening pedestrian rush hour. Then again, she might take the Tube or a taxi, or an Uber home. Or not even live around here. Or she may have been here just as tourist with her family. They all thought she resided in London, that her parents were visiting. But why did they so readily conclude that? A helpful surmise based on an overheard conversation, but if not true, one that would make the search more endless.

She had her picture of the savior. She stared at it intently. Finally, she grabbed an iced tea. A large one, and sat on a bench near the London Bridge. The same bench near the trash bin where she saw the hospital smock.

I will wait here.

Becca put on some suntan lotion. It was not hot, but the sun was glorious and tanning. She was patient today. She periodically searched the web for stories on the healing King, Atlantis, Winston, the lottery winner, Jay Jones. Finally, a new story popped up.

A man, formerly blind, had set up a new company and had just received substantial funding from a first-round venture capital round of financing. His company had already filed patents and claimed to have ground breaking technology in restoring vision to those who had lost vision from accidents. The technology was stated to be promising for other blindness, including persons born blind. The British government had even often offered a generous incentives program at the national and local levels in the form of subsidies and tax incentives and abatements. The national health institute made an impromptu grant. It was potentially historic. The founder, a man named John Masterson, stated he had recently regained his vision. It was a miracle, is all he would say. Some speculate it was his own technology that provided the miracle. His mother was vicepresident in charge of charitable operations, the division in charge of caring for the needy and poor, who could not afford the procedures, once the prototypes were approved and in use in the marketplace. She, too, it was rumored, had recovered from a serious illness.

Becca scribbled down notes from the article. John Masterson was on her list. Her invitation list, too. She started to put together her list. She had names of thirty people from the play. She had the names of the four kids healed in Hyde Park, including Shaylee Smith and her mother, Merle Smith. All four mothers would be invited. The two nurses would be invited. She had not talked to them, but Merle had sent their contact information to her. She would invite them over the phone first. They had kept quiet. There was Amanda Worthington, her college best friend, and Mark Buckingham. Her Aunt Grace. Jay Jones and James Tudor. Now, John Masterson and his mother. The London Bridge jumper, an Alfred Jackman and his wife. The guard at Windsor Castle. The Queen's cousin, Charles of North Hampton, and Abigail Johnstone, the shipping heiress. Johanna and Savannah Stark. Jackson, the dog. The lottery winner, Houston Garrison. Chauncey Parsons. His friend, Pete Copperfield and his wife. She had finally met him. He had told his story to her. Another leading lady of British Society, Grace Bennington, and her two granddaughters. Chauncey had called and told her about the bizarre incident at Primrose, information he had garnered from his friends serving that area. And the savior/hero. *Where are you, my dear? And, of course, Winston, his wife and daughter!*

The man with no hunch in his back had watched Becca for most of the afternoon, after he had first spotted her trolling the Riverwalk. He admired her beauty and grace. He had recently read as much as he could about her, hearing that she was investigating the case. He was excited to meet her, but felt intimidated. He had to work the night shift at the hospital by 4:00 P.M. So, it was now or later. Soon, a little girl joined him. It was the orphan girl, that the King had healed at his request. Her name was Rose. That is what he called her. Her real name did not matter to him.

Becca sensed energy. It was similar to the energy she felt from Jackson. She looked up. Soon she saw the pretty eyes of a little girl nestled upon her. The little girl smiled brightly when Becca looker her way. She curtsied, and waved. Becca waved back. Tingling went down Becca's back when her eyes drifted to the man standing next to the little girl. It was him. The hero, the savior. He waved, too. Becca beckoned them to the bench.

"And whom do I have the pleasure of meeting?"

"I am Bart Tower. I think you already know who I am! This is Rose Hathaway."

Bart at that moment had given Rose the last name of Shakespeare's wife.

"I see. You are the hero of Tower Bridge."

Bart looked around to see if there were any television or newspaper cameras. Then he looked for smartphones aimed his way. Nothing.

"I lived here for about ten years. Under this bench. I was a top shelf beggar. No pride in that. I had a severely hunched back. I was known as the hunchback of London Bridge. I spent many nights in jail and in shelters. Sometimes, a local merchant would offer me employment. But I never held a job. I would fight back when people laughed at me. But for the last three years, I have had visions of an American elder statesman, coming to London, to heal me. Last weekend, I felt his enormous presence. Then, as I slept, he appeared in my dreams. Or I saw his spirit, I am not sure which. I begged him, in my most effective way, to heal me. I awoke that night, actually, it was around midnight, and there he was, standing next to me. He healed me. He said he was the King of Atlantis. He told me to serve the common good."

"And Rose?"

"I was about to die. I was going to hospice. I have no family. Bart had taken a job at my hospital. He liked me. He told me about a King. I thought it was a fairy tale. I came with him to the bench. And the King was real. He healed me, too! And now, Bart is my guardian, or he will be soon. A wealthy barrister volunteered to help with the legal process. I am so happy!" the young girl smiled, wearing a nice fall dress with a floral pattern, and a headband in her new long flowing hair.

"How did you save the jumper?"

"I was with the King. We saw the commotion and the jumper. I did not want the King to risk his life. I once was a good swimmer. I just jumped in to save him. The King did not heal him. I saved the man. But I think the King may have saved me again. My lungs were filled with water. He left. So, did I. But I know there were videos of my rescue effort. I have avoided the press, so far. And no one has figured out that I was man with a hunch in his back," Bart looked to the ground, remembering his dirty blanket.

"You will be part of my story, or tale, if that is fine with the two of you?"

They both nodded in Agreement.

"And there will be a royal ball or gala, to celebrate the engagement of the Queen's cousin. We hope to invite the King! We will invite the two of you, and others that were healed. It is really a gala for the King! But that is a secret!"

"My lips are sealed with wax!" the little girl Rose laughed, and pressed an imaginary seal on her lips. Bart laughed and did the same.

"I will invite the jumper and his wife, as well. They were back together in no time. She must be so patient, and must not have ever fallen out of love with him."

"Maybe someday I will find love," Bart lamented.

"I know I will," Rose smiled, looking at the river, and then St. Paul's Cathedral.

"And me, too!" Becca added, looking somewhat unsure as she blurted it out.

They all placed their hands together, as if to make a pact.

Becca left. Bart went back to work. Rose eagerly did her homework on her new computer, donated by the barrister.

16.

BECCA SAT across the table from John Masterson, on Tuesday morning. He was wide eyed and cheery. He smiled effusively at Becca. She was a little unnerved by his adoration of her. Although he was handsome, she did not find him to be her type. But she let him admire her. At least it was a compliment.

John told his story. Becca was blown away by his understanding of image technology. He had studied industrial and medical imaging, and photoelectric science over the years. But it was the vision he had the night after he was healed, where it all came so clear to him. He quickly had filed patents, with the aid of London's top tier intellectual property firm. He made contacts with leading venture firms, who snapped up stock in his company in a first-round financing in just days. He and his company were on the fast pace to bring the technology to prototype, and test it on blind people in need.

Becca took copious notes.

"Did you tell your investors about the King?"

"I did not. I mentioned I had a vision. But they did not know that I was ever blind. I did not tell them. I was a street person, so they did not know me. My patents were so valuable, that they did no due diligence on me personally. They did not care. I have no criminal record, and my blindness was not at birth, so there is no record of my blindness. They are running the business now, with trained executives, a CEO, a CTO, a CFO and project managers. I am the President. But I am not doing much for the company. But I do own voting control, and over half of the stock, fully diluted. My barrister protected me. The investors do not have a preferred equity. Their stock is the same as mind. And there is a good shareholder's agreement that protects me. My role is to get the product to market, to help as many blind people as we can. I will keep some of my gains, when the stock is sold. But most I will give to charity."

"Amanda says there may have been a girl you were interested in?"

"How about you?"

"Oh, I am not on the market!"

"Yes, I figured you were still smitten with Chester Jones! And Amanda told me about the three of you, and your intricate relationships! By the way, I think Jay Jones is Chester Jones, and that the King must have healed him. I heard him talking on the Riverwalk to his friend. He and James Tudor never paid any attention to me, the blind man. They must have thought I was deaf, too. But I knew it was him, and that he had no legs. When I watched the game, and of course, you, on television, I guessed it was Chester because Chester hung out on the Riverwalk right near where I was healed. I am pretty sure, you know. Well, the girl, Jenny Smithson, left for America. She is getting her PHD at NYU in international relations. She is gone. I dated her in college. But once I went blind, I dumped her in self-pity. She was devastated. She cared not about my infirmity. I regret that decision."

"Does she know you are healed?"

"No, I don't have her contacts. Because I was blind, I was not on social media. I don't know. But I am happy. And Amanda is nice. But she is my friend. She and I want to keep it that way."

"I see. Hmmm, on Amanda!"

"Honestly, we are not a match! We will go to each other's wedding someday. It is nice to have a woman friend. We had nice conversations over the years. We both had so much, before we had our afflictions. And now we are both healed."

Becca nodded in understanding.

"Did you have visions, dreams, or intuition about the King before he arrived?"

"I had visions of him, once or twice. But the night he healed me, I saw his spirit first. Then he came in person. I felt his energy from afar. He healed others that Saturday night. I saw a few others healed, at least four more. I know he healed the man with the hunch back first. I saw that in my dreams, and I saw him with no hunch in his back, after I was healed. I knew the man with the hunch back. He let me feel it. We were fellow men of the streets."

John Masterson, looked sullen as he remembered his dark years. But in some respect, he missed the comradery of the people on the street.

Becca timely chimed in.

"We are having a gala party at Kensington Palace to celebrate the engagement of the Queen's cousin. But it is really a celebration, reception, and reunion for the King and his flock, his healed people. You will be invited. Your friend, the man who no longer has a hunch in his back, his name is Bart Tower, he will be invited, as will Amanda and Mark. You can see your old friends. And your Mum is invited! I will send you the details, once finalized."

John looked up from his desk. His eyes glistened.

"I am so grateful. Were you reading my mind?"

"Only your body language, and I read people pretty well, too."

Becca shook his hand, and two said so long for now.

17.

WINSTON HAILED a cab from Heathrow on Wednesday. His British Airways flight was smooth. His cab took about an hour to reach Southwark. Elizabeth was there to meet him.

The weather was overcast and cool. It was early evening, and the sun was set. Winston told Elizabeth to sit down. It now was eleven days since he, as the former King of Atlantis, had embarked on his healing spree.

"I have something to tell you, Elizabeth. You are probably wondering why I have returned so quickly."

"My God, are you ok?" Elizabeth lamented, leaning forward in concern, and pressing her hand on top of her father's hand.

Winston smiled in a fatherly, and comforting way. "I am indeed ok! And even better than ok!"

"That is good. I have a feeling on what you might say," she said cautiously, but expectantly. She rested back against the couch and crossed her arms in front of her. She was wearing sweat pants and a light wool sweater for an autumn day.

"While I was in London I was overcome with a powerful energy. I had visions from my past. My deep past. I cannot explain it. But I believe I was once a healer, in fact, the Supreme Priest, in Atlantis, the legendary lost continent. And later the King. I may have been King when it crashed forever into the ocean. But the power to heal transcends time and space and came back to me. With that power and guided by that vision, I healed many people in London on our visit. I don't know most of them, but I know the names of a few of them and read about a few more of them. I believe that the source of my power may be some energy crystals left over from Atlantis and brought to foreign shores before the final demise of the continent. I believe they are in England and in London. I believe their power can be tapped into by people like me that are highly elevated in their conscious realms, as I certainly was as Supreme Priest of Atlantis. I am here to study and research what I can find. The source is near the Thames River. The energy flow can travel through water around the world. I tapped into it on the Connecticut River to heal some friends in need. You know them, Saint Nick, Sir Richard, and Donny Boy. Maybe I can heal more people."

Winston sat back and took a sip of his English hot tea. He did not take his eyes off of his daughter. He was wearing khaki slacks and a vineyard vines button down light blue shirt, along with his boat shoes with no socks. His light dark blue jacket was on the armrest of the couch, ready for the next journey. He smiled broadly. Elizabeth was speechless. Her mouth was agape.

"I want to meet the Queen. After all I am royalty, too! I tried to meet her at Windsor Castle, but the guards escorted me out, thinking I was a crazy old man! Although they treated me respectfully."

"Is that why my knee and back are fine now? When was I healed by you? And the play? People were silly and giddy. I heard a man say that he was healed. And the maintenance guy at Greenwich Park? He won the lottery! Was he the one that drove us? Were you the one he talked about? And the London Bridge Jumper? Oh God, not Chester Jones, too! Is that why they were singing in the train about him? This is unbelievable! What are we to do? Does Mum know? Anne?"

Elizabeth leaned forward and put her face in her hands.

"I have heard rumors of a King healing people during the time of your stay. Honestly, the thought occurred to me that it may have been you!

"I heard that London's best investigative reporter is looking into this. But oddly, no one has stepped forward to the press. And the press won't report this. There was some social media on this as people are wondering how Chester Jones was healed so quickly. But it is random."

"Let us get ahold of this reporter. What paper is she with?"

"London's leading newspaper. I will do it first thing in the morning."

With that they both retired for the evening. Across London, many people were restless. They felt something, something deep in their souls. Energy inside of them stirred.

The next morning, Thursday, Elizabeth searched the web for contact information for Becca Hollingsworth. She found it and placed a call. She left a voicemail, as dictated by her father.

"I am the daughter of the man you have been looking for. He is in London. We should meet! It could be a royal affair. I look forward to hearing from you. Regards, Elizabeth Churchill."

The next morning Elizabeth grabbed her light wool sweater and put in on. She grabbed a bright blue windbreaker, and wrapped it over her shoulders. Winston had put on one of his fine golf outfits, with Under Armour navy blue long pants, and a Under Armour blue pullover, with horizontal pleats. They both brought a bag for their shoes.

Off they went to Royal Birkdale in Southport for the day. It was about three and one half hours to get there by train. They arrived and rented golf clubs.

"This was the venue for this year's Open. That was such an exciting tournament. Next year I want to attend Wimbledon and the Open."

Elizabeth looked proudly at her father. She was still overwhelmed at his confession of greatness. She was so happy for her Mum and herself that they were healed. Anne had been healed of her nagging injuries from collegiate athletics. She and Anne were texting furiously the entire train ride. Anne had kept the secret until Winston had told her in person. They were giddy.

An older man, beaten by the weather and the years, was their caddy. He was a magnificent caddy. He knew all the tricks, and knew the greens oh so well. He figured out both of their golf swings after a couple of holes, and clubbed them perfectly. The day was overcast and chilly. Winston carded a smooth 41 on the front. Elizabeth, a college athlete, broke 50 and was ecstatic.

The caddy seemed to study Winston intently. He was a professional observer of people. On the fourteenth tee, he grabbed Winston by the shoulder blade and whispered into his ear.

"Who are you, Sir? Honestly, I sense greatness!"

Winston looked back at him with a smile. The energy within him started to swell. He saw the caddy's aura. There were so many holes in it.

"After the round, meet me at the pub on the main road. I can help you."

The caddy had a hop in his step the final few holes. Winston made par on the final five holes to card a 79. He was ecstatic. Elizabeth carded a 96, and was very pleased.

A half hour later, Winston found the caddy outside of the pub. He was with his two granddaughters. Both were stricken and ill, and looked like life was a terror for them. They cracked the slightest of smiles when they saw the eyes of Winston, so deeply blue and distant. Elizabeth arrived. She saw the scene. She waited to witness the action. Her heart pounded.

Winston grabbed the hands of the two girls and their grandfather.

"I am the once and former King of Atlantis. Upon my word, you shall be healed. So, it shall be said, so, it shall be done. You are hereby healed. Go, and serve the common good."

The caddy leaned forward and picked up his two granddaughters. He could not believe his now brightly lit eyes. Gone were the deep gray hollows in his eyes of years of drinking and depression. His back was fine. His throbbing knees seemed spring-like. But mostly, he saw two angelic little girls with bright beaming pink faces, freed from the tyranny of their disease. They were free at last from their shackles of pain and suffering.

"Long Live the King!" the caddy cried. When he turned to hug Winston, he was gone.

Three hours later they arrived at her flat in Central London, Elizabeth broke the silence of the last few hours.

"Dad, I don't know what to say. I am a believer. Where do you go from here? What will you do now? Who will you heal? Where will you live? Will you go public? That could change your life so dramatically?"

Winston sat reflectively. He smiled, though, thinking of the angelic faces of the two happy little girls.

"I got the name of the caddy at the course. Just in case, we need it. He called his girls by name when we left. Joss and Jess. They were so cute. Maybe future golfers?"

"Maybe."

"I have not checked my smartphone all day. I wanted to enjoy your company, before the world goes crazy for us. Let me check the news sites first," Elizabeth puckered her lips in concern.

She checked all the lead news sites. No articles on Winston, the King of Atlantis, or even the caddy in Southport. She then checked her email and texts. There were many, and there was one from Becca Hollingsworth.

"Elizabeth Churchill! I cannot believe I have heard from you! Is your father really Winston Churchill! How ironic! Is he both the former King of Atlantis and the former Prime Minister of the United Kingdom? Omigod! I would love to meet you and of course your father. I have met so many of those that he blessed with his healing. Did you see my story in the paper on Monday or on our website? It was about the gala party for the Queen's cousin and his new paramour and shipping heiress. The party date is not set. I intended a message for your father, the King. It was subtle, but hopefully, for him, quite discernible. I wrote, 'Romeo and Juliet, where are thou? Surely, you want to attend? The hunchback from Notre Dame is no longer, and London Bridge is not falling down, and Humpty Dumpty was put back together again, and the prime meridian is still secure, and Mary Poppins has flown her kite. One now sees the light. English football still stirs the night. And the statute of Winston Churchill stands guard to keep things right. This shall be a gala fit for queens and kings, Princes and Princesses. King Arthur would be proud.' Let me know when to meet. I shall be very discreet. I have not told the Queen or her secretary as of yet. Best Regards, BH".

"I did not read or see that. Surely, now, I see the clues. The play on Sunday night at the Playhouse, where so many were healed, the man with a hunch in his back, now healed and normal in his stance, the man who jumped from London Bridge and lived, the grandmother and her daughters in Primrose, where Mary flew her kite. The reference to Winston, of course. The reference to a King. There was a fellow at the Tate museum who said he was a former football player. The blind man sees again. Yes, I may have discerned her message, if I had read it."

"Should I respond to her? What should I say? Where should we meet? Should I tell her your real name? The football player is probably Chester Jones. Everyone is bedazzled by his play and stunned by his comeback. Most think he did it through secret intensive rehabilitation. Now we know it was you!"

Winston wanted to meet this Becca. That he was invited to a party with the Queen stunned him. He wanted to meet her. Maybe she knew something, as Monarch, something passed down from the ages. He suspected that England somehow was once a part of Atlantis. Maybe there were secretive or lingering ties, or legends or myths, or knowledge. He had to know. From his own experience, he felt enormous energy emanating from the city.

"Tell her to meet us Friday morning. She knows about the man with a hunch back. Tell her to meet us at London Bridge, in the small park at the bench. She should know where it is. Do you know what she looks like?"

"I do."

"The football player may have been one of three chaps I healed at the Tate museum. Two were without legs, and in wheelchairs. No rehabilitation for him. Maybe he is not Chester Jones, if Chester Jones had legs to rehabilitate."

"Dad, Mum and I were there at most of the miraculous healings. How did we not know? Was it really you. Of course, it was. I am healed. I witnessed you heal the caddy and his girls. This is so amazing. I am sorry I needed to witness the healings first hand to believe you. But I did believe. I did."

"It is fine. I love you dearly, as I do Mary and Anne. Maybe you were in Atlantis, too. Maybe a Princess! Who knows. Maybe you were a priestess, and someday will discover the innate power to heal, or how to access this energy source to heal," Winston calmly addressed her, as she rested in ease.

Elizabeth thought deeply about her potential. Then she drifted back to the present. She needed to shower. But first, an email to Becca.

"Meet us tomorrow at 10:00 A.M. at London Bridge, at the park bench. Dad said you would know where it is! I have blonde hair, and am tall, and will wear a white wind breaker, and blue jeans and flats. Winston likely will wear khaki pants, Nike sneakers, and a golf cap. Looking forward to meeting one of London's finest citizens!"

Winston called Mary. He told them to catch a flight to London tomorrow, Friday. He was going to push for a party date on Saturday night. He did not want to wait long to meet the Queen.

Becca read the email. She started to hyperventilate. She was going to meet the King. She might be healed! She might have one of the biggest stories in years, at least one of the biggest feel good stories. She was overwhelmed with nervousness. She thought of bringing her Aunt Grace. After an hour, she realized she had not responded. Panic set in. Was it too late.

"Yes, I will meet you! I will be wearing a light wool suit and white blouse and designer shoes. I am on business, of course."

A minute later she was in a frenzy.

"No, I will wear jeans and windbreaker, too! It may be chilly, yet all sunshine!"

Elizabeth read the emails and chuckled. *I think I will have a new friend. Maybe she was lead citizen in Atlantis, too. Oh, such folly, Dad! But wait, it must be true! What must I do to totally believe.*

18.

ECCA WAS SITTING on the park bench when they arrived. She was radiant. Her hair was shining brightly in the sun. Her cheeks were flushed pink, her lips full and polished with lipstick. Her posture was erect. She held a single daisy in her hand. Her jeans were loose fitting and not designer. She wore sneakers with peds for socks. She wore a white windbreaker. She was tall. She could pass as a sister for Elizabeth, with only the slight red tint to her hair differing from Elizabeth's golden blond locks. Both woman wore their hair down today in pony tails. Winston was amused at their similarity in appearance. It made him relax. Another daughter, was his thought. Becca lost her nervousness on seeing the father and daughter. She saw Bart Tower snickering over yonder behind a tree. He had given her the daisy. She liked it a lot.

Elizabeth approached her first. There was an instant bond and friendship. They both smiled and then laughed. After the mandatory salutations and introductions, Elizabeth waived her Dad over. He had spotted Bart, and had waved to him. Becca's heart raced, the recognition confirming her belief that this was the King.

Winston approached her. He had plenty of misgivings about meeting with a reporter. But he thought it was his best shot at meeting the Queen.

"Good morning Ms. Hollingsworth. I am Josh Churchill."

Becca was a good reader of people. She knew right away that Winston was a kind man. She sensed his anxiety about her status as a beat reporter.

"I am Becca. You can call me Becca. I am awe struck at meeting you, Your Grace! Are you not Winston?" She bowed, not knowing quite what to do, and uncertain about his new name.

"Winston is my nickname. You might guess why! Got the nickname in college and it stuck, except at work. I hear you are having a party for the Queen's cousin. Will the Queen be in attendance?"

"Yes, of course. And we would like to invite you and Elizabeth, too."

"And what of my wife Mary, and other daughter Anne. May they attend as well? They are flying in tonight. We are all flying back to the states early next week, I suspect, but that is not firm."

Winston glanced around to see if there were any cameras, or observers, other than Bart, who stepped away, apparently. It was a normal day. No one paid heed of them, even with a well-known reporter on hand. Winston marveled at how pretty Becca was, more as an observer, and not with any thoughts in his heart. But soon he saw her aura, and her dark spots and her evident heartache and sadness. He knew she was in casual clothes now, to meet him, the King and healer, not as a reporter, but as a person in need. The instant camaraderie between Becca and his daughter confirmed his conclusions. He smiled at Becca in a paternal way.

"Have a seat on the bench, Becca," he summoned her, waving his golf hat now in his hand toward the magical bench. She started to say something, but stammered out only a guttural noise. He held her hand, at her uncontrolled utterance, easing her softly onto the bench. Soon Bart was nearby. She gave him the slightest of smiles. She was apprehensive and nervous. She started to breathe heavily. She thought she was going to faint. Elizabeth sat next to her, and rested her arm over her shoulder.

"You will be fine. Look at the white clouds that just popped up over the horizon. They look like a Castle and a Temple! My Dad told me about the clouds! You are about to be healed. Relax. Take a deep breath. You are fine," Elizabeth spoke softly and soothingly. She seemed to know that Becca would soon be a new friend. Bart came over and joined the action. He patted her on the back, if not a bit too gruffly. Elizabeth did not know him, but suspected it was the man with a hunch back, that no longer had a hunch back. Her father had told her about all of his healings.

Bart and Elizabeth stepped away. Winston stepped near her.

Becca blurted out, "Yes, Mary and Anne can come. Let's have the party tomorrow night. Everyone that is invited, is on standby. We were just waiting for you, Your Grace!"

Winston stepped back. He stared at Becca, as he was about to go into a trance like state to summon his internal energy. He nodded at her answer, and then looked deep into his soul for the energy needed to heal Becca. At first there was nothing. Bart scratched his head. Elizabeth folded her arms. Winston searched harder. He did not feel the energy. He knew he found it the day before in Southport. He was puzzled.

"Becca, let's walk to the river."

Becca stood up. She started to panic. Was all of the King's energy used up? Was the fairy tale over? Why bother with a story that had ended? She grabbed Winston's hands and stared deeply into his eyes, searching for magic, searching for answers, hoping for miracles.

A chill wind gusted up from the river. The familiar feel of surging energy returned. Winston grabbed Becca's soft hands into his, and gazed deeply back into her eyes. All that she saw was the deepest blue eyes she had ever seen. She trembled again, and barely stood.

"I am the once and former King of Atlantis. Upon my word, you shall be healed. So, it shall be said, so, it shall be done. You are hereby healed. Go, and serve the common good."

"Long Live the King!" She shouted with all of her might. Soon Bart and Elizabeth joined in the chorus. They heard the soft voice of a young girl join the chorus as well. It was Rose, the young girl Bart now cared for. She had returned from school, certainly tipped off by Bart.

Becca broke down into tears, she was so happy. She hugged Winston for a long time and then kissed him on the cheek. She sat back down on the bench.

Winston sat next to her.

"And you are going to write a Tale, I have heard? What do you know?"

"I will not write anything if you don't want me to."

"We will see. And there may be a way to write a Tale, without disclosing my identity. What do you know?"

"I know quite a lot. Should I start?" She said, now quite calm.

"Yes. I do not know the names of the people that were healed, save a few, like Bart. I surmise you know about the blind man, the two children saved in Primrose, the London

Bridge jumper, saved by Bart, the football player. I have discerned this from your invitation."

Bart and Rose left. They wanted to give Becca privacy. Elizabeth said she would take mental notes.

"I don't know the order of your miracles, but I know many that happened. I know the phrase that you use. I may want to know more about Atlantis, about the energy that I felt, the light that I saw, the visions I had last night, the love I feel for you, more like a daughter or niece, your life and soul history, what lies in the future."

"Ok. But what of the Tale itself."

"Well, as best as I can surmise, on Saturday night, you healed the blind man. His name is John Masterson. I met with him. He is now an entrepreneur with venture capital backing for his innovative discoveries in eye replacements and vision repair, using sophisticated imaging technology. He says his technology is a vital third cog to genetic engineering and stem cell processes underway now in vision restoration. Bart was healed Saturday, too."

Winston responded, eagerly. "There were others on Saturday night. A woman with cancer, an elder man stricken with horrific arthritis, a young girl, who had lost her hand in a boating accident, and an escaped patient from the local mental health hospital. I do not know any of their names. And I had a vision. I visited the blind man, a girl in Mayfair, and two soldiers in a soldier's home. It was if I was really there. And I sense they saw me, as well, in their dreams or mind's eye."

Bart scratched his chin. He now was clean shaven, and had thick brown hair, combed back, as if he were a banker.

"Yes, I saw him in a vision that night. But in many more in years past. And, I know this Riverwalk and its people better than anyone. I think I can find all three of them. I know the girl with the missing hand, by face. I can find her. I will find them. I am sure," Bart brushed his hair back, feeling important and germane to the mission of a full attendance list.

Becca continued. "On Sunday, you had quite a day. You healed my friend, Amanda Worthington, my best friend!"

"I am touched by that revelation. Must be serendipity. Amazing coincidence. Wow. She was the burn victim. The one I saw in Mayfair. And I healed a little boy, who was with her, and the blind man's mother."

Becca was pleased with her investigative aptitude and success. "The boy's name is Mark Buckingham. He now resides with Amanda and her parents. You should see Amanda's painting! It is magnificent. I think it is Atlantis! The Palace and the Temple. You will absolutely love it."

Winston leaned back and looked at the two clouds. They still retained their shape, at least to him. "Yes, I would love to see her painting, and to meet her again."

"You and your family later went to the department store. I saw you there!"

"This is truly amazing. Yes, I remember. You were very professionally attired. My wife and I admired you! I admit, I noticed you! My wife agreed with me on your excellent appearance, and professional ambience and confident nature. And we were correct!"

"Indeed, and thank you! Your Grace, I am humble to be here on the bench with you and your daughter," Becca straightened her back and took a deep breath.

"Well, you next healed the candy clerk at the department store. She is Abigail Johnstone, a shipping heiress of tremendous wealth. She was suffering from late stage Alzheimer's. Her fiancé is Charles Wingate, of North Hampton, second cousin to the Queen. The gala party is to celebrate their engagement, at least as a cover story! It is really for you and all the people you healed and saved!" Becca started to cry, as tears streamed down her cheeks. Elizabeth, sitting to her left, held her hand in support. Winston, sitting to her right took off his golf cap and put it on her head. She started to laugh at that gesture. Elizabeth laughed, too. Then Bart and Rose laughed.

"I so much want to meet all of them. And the Queen, too," Winston spoke, revealing his real reason for the visit back to London.

"I want to talk to her about the Crown's knowledge of legends and lore, and Atlantis, and energy fields, and energy crystals, and anything she can tell me. Maybe there is science to the healing. It would be nice to find that out for the world," Winston gazed back at the two clouds once again. Soon, the clouds would be gone, as larger overcast clouds were threatening to cover the blue sky.

"I will make certain you have a private audience with the Queen prior to the party."

"Very well."

Becca did not need her notes, they were vivid in her mind. She had even drafted a first draft of her Tale, with blanks for the anticipated missing links.

"Next stop was Hyde Park, which is near the famous department store. Four children, all terminally ill, were healed by you. And their two nurses. My reference to Mary Poppins flying a kite was for these four kids. They and their Mums are all coming to the gala party. I spend considerable time with Shaylee Smith, a young girl healed that day, and her Mum, Merle Smith. She put me in touch with the other three children and their Mums."

"Excellent. I want to meet them and talk to them about their futures."

"The next stop was indeed extraordinary. What a place to heal so many. "Romeo and Juliet! How romantic, how historical, and how special. My Aunt Grace was at the play. She told me much."

Becca stopped suddenly, and then looked at Winston in the eyes.

"Oh, yes, Winston. A nickname, eh! Makes sense. The Queen has been looking for you, too, you know. We gathered Winston might be your name! I heard your wife call you Winston. Then, as you might expect, when you were escorted from Windsor Castle there was ample video of you and your family. The Queen has worked with me to find you. She showed me the video. I knew it was you, Winston. We checked databases, and flight lists, but came up empty. Now, we know why. The Queen will be pleased that her intelligence resources were not lacking after all!" Becca smiled, pleased that she was sharing classified and important information to Winston as well.

"You continue to overwhelm me! I am pleased the Queen wants to meet the King!"

"Long Live the King," Bart yelled.

"Why do the healed persons say that? Usually, that is said when the old King passes away, and there is a new King," Elizabeth asked.

"I believe that the King of Atlantis died with his continent, when it crashed into the sea. I had visions of that catastrophic event. And I, the former King, have returned to the present as the new King. Of what, I am not sure. Maybe I am King for the former citizens of that great continent who have returned for a second chance. Maybe each of you was a citizen of Atlantis."

There was silence. They all contemplated his words. Winston broke the silence.

"You would not know this. But I healed Mary and Elizabeth on Sunday morning, before I went out. They were asleep. They did not know that I healed them. It was, in a way, comical, as they felt better, could not explain it, and determined that it was not likely true or lasting!"

Elizabeth laughed and confirmed her Dad's conclusions.

"Before we went to the play, we stopped in Camden. I healed a young musician. He started to play a new tune. He sang about "Lovin' in Camden" to a country-jazz-rap like beat. Very creative. He had a name on his guitar case. It was Branden Dunster."

"You have got to be kidding me!" Elizabeth shrieked.

"Yes, for sure," Becca screamed.

"What?" Winston asked dumbly.

"That song is number one on all the charts. It falls under so many genres, it is just number one on all of the billboard charts! He has a new album to be released on October 31!"

"Amazing. I think he saw the notes in the sky!"

Elizabeth moved the Tale forward. "We went to the Tate museum in the morning on Sunday. You were gone for long periods of time, Dad," Elizabeth questioned her Dad.

"Yes, Becca, this may interest you. You referenced a football player. He may have been at the museum. I first healed an Australian surfer. He had lost his arm, likely in a shark attack. I healed the two men I had seen in the soldier's home in my vision on Saturday night. We brought them outside to the Riverwalk, near the bank of the river. They were asleep, but awoke later. One was a football player, and maybe also a soldier, the other, I believe a soldier. They were close friends."

Becca's eyes had widened. Heart pounded again.

"Did the football player have no legs?"

"Correct. That is why I am not sure if he is the Chester Jones of current fame."

"James Tudor is the soldier, and Chester's childhood best friend. James Tudor has not showed up. We are still searching for him. The football player is definitely Chester Jones.

He recovered his legs not by rehabilitation, but by your miraculous healing! I confirmed this with the soldier's home."

Becca sniffled and bit her lip.

"There is more. I once loved him. I may still, I don't know. Chester left me because he loved or wanted Amanda. She did not want to see him while I was his girlfriend. So, he dumped me for her. But she never went out with him, at least not that I know of. And then, the fire, and he dropped her, too."

Becca continued, talking to the river, as much as her bench mates.

"Yesterday, I talked further with Amanda. Amanda told me she walked by two men in wheel chairs by the Riverwalk the Saturday before the Sunday that you healed her. She noticed they were checking her out. But then they saw her hideous face and snickered and mocked her beneath their breath. But she heard them. The little boy told her she was pretty to cheer her up. She gave him a daisy in gratitude. He gave it to the blind man. She wonders whether they are James and Chester. It appears that they are."

Becca drew a deep breath.

"But Chester Jones is great again. And he is serving the common good. He gave a substantial sum of money to the soldier's home. I think he has changed. But he hurt me deeply, once, and his scorn of Amanda on last Saturday, was so terrible an act, I can still feel her pain."

Elizabeth held her hand again.

"I think you should talk to him at the gala party. You will know your feelings for him then, and if he has any for you. There certainly are so many men in London that would love to court you! And if he and Amanda are destined for one another, so be it. Keep her as your dear friend. It sounds as if she was loyal to you, years ago."

"Yes, I think so."

Bart piped in, without the chivalry of a Prince. "I certainly will dance with you tomorrow!"

"Bart, I think not! But, I will always think of you as a friend," Becca mewed.

Rose said her two pence, too.

"Oh, and I thought there was a chance you would be my Mum!"

Becca immediately flashed back to her healing. *Mum, I can be a Mum.*

She cried again out loud for a few moments. Winston knew why. He had seen it in her aura. The others were not sure, and thought it had to do with Amanda and Chester.

"And what of Manic Monday?" Winston moved the conversation forward.

"The Greenwich events are truly death defying! I spoke with Chauncey Parsons. He was the medic who came to save you and the maintenance worker. He showed me the split tree! And the burned-out cart. And the maintenance man, he used his divine intervention from you and/or the lightning, to win the lottery. His name is Houston Garrison. But the most gripping story may be about the dog!"

Elizabeth chimed in.

"He was so cute. And he got his fourth leg back and ran with the other two dogs!

"Johanna and Savannah Stark. They were the Mum and daughter. I talked to them. The dog's name was Jackson."

"Yes, I saw the love in Elizabeth's eyes for the dog. I was glad to help him. The lightning strike was not my doing. I am not Thor! But the natural energy was enormous. I contemplate even now that the enormity of the energy storm, may have related to me, and my access to some energy source, whether a universal source, internal source, natural source, or crystalline source from Atlantis. I just do not have an answer."

"Is there anything else on Manic Monday?"

Dad, we went to Primrose Park, too. Did you have something to do with that car accident?" Elizabeth asked, thinking back to the glorious day at the park.

"Yes, I did. A woman had run over two little girls. I saved them. The woman passed. She wanted to pass. She was ready. Another woman held the girls. Maybe a grandmother," Winston recalled, sad that the one woman had wanted to pass on.

Becca perked up again.

"That was Grace Bennington, a British matriarch and society member. Those were her two granddaughters, Starr and Sensa. I heard about the event from Chauncey. His cohorts were suspicious of their findings of two healthy girls at the scene of the accident, given the rumors of healing and a King. Grace is quite grateful of the King and his actions. The other woman was her cousin."

"You have done fabulous detective work, Becca. On to Tuesday. I have nothing more. Other than that Houston probably received his divine wisdom of the lottery system from me, not the lightning. I hope he serves the common good."

"Well, Tuesday, we have covered, I believe. It is when you went to Windsor Castle. You healed a guard, we know. Bart, and you, saved the London Bridge jumper. He has reunited with his wife, and repaid his debts. I know you are aware of that. Anything else? Oh, I forgot. Rose! She was healed on Tuesday."

"That is good for now. On Sunday morning, before I saw Amanda, Mark and the blind man, I healed a young lad, as well, without the chant. Not sure, how though."

"Dad, what of Westminster? And Southport?"

"I did not hear that you attended Westminster Abbey. Did you bring any kings and queens or famous scientists or poets or playwrights to life?" Becca squeamishly asked, fearing a whole new level to Winston's powers.

"Who would be King or Queen if King Henry VIII was resurrected?" Elizabeth calmly asked, as if a student asking a question of a political science professor.

Becca laughed recognizing the absurdity of her fears.

"I have not resurrected any one, nor do I believe that I have that power, or that the Atlanteans had that power. I can assure you of that. So, there will be no issues of the right to the throne!"

Elizabeth, wanting to be scholarly, added, "I believe that once you have died, you are no longer in succession for the throne. No predecessors are permitted in the succession line of Kings and Queens! That is my legal conclusion. Ha!"

"That makes sense," Becca concurred.

Winston stood.

"We must go and get ready to pick up Mary and Anne. Becca let us know about the party. AND keep me informed about the status of your Tale!"

"And what to wear!"

"I will. I shall! And what of Southport, and is there anything else about Westminster?"

"He healed a caddy and his two grandchildren, Joss and Jess in Southport. We had played golf yesterday in Southport. At Royal Birkdale. The Caddy was Peter McAlister."

"I will find them," Becca stated.

"Westminster, that is our home town in Connecticut. My Dad healed some of his golf friends."

"Well, we can have a stateside gala party later."

They hugged and left for their continued duties.

19.

THE QUEEN sat upright in her straight back wooden chair behind her desk. She was relaxed. She had met royalty before from other countries, and heads of state. She had not met a King from ancient times. Still she was relaxed and intensely interested in the man that sat across from her.

Winston was fascinated with the Queen. She was modern royalty, and he was eager to converse with the long-standing monarch. He was wearing a fine men's navy blue suit-one that he bought at one of London's finest men's clothing store. Even his shoes, shirt, tie, belt and socks were the finest. The Queen was in her professional attire as well. She looked splendid. They both felt a powerful vibe. Winston felt enormous energy welling up inside him. Winston broke the peaceful silence.

"Your Grace, is our meeting under surveillance? For posterity, I suppose," Winston spoke, while momentarily crossing his arms across his chest.

The Queen saw his protective measure, but had already made her decision.

"I have elected to keep our discussion private. No video, audio or any type of digital surveillance. I would not want hackers to view or read our conversation today. And we have swept the office for electronic eavesdroppers! Rest assured, Your Grace," the Queen slightly bowed her head.

Winston dropped his arms to his lap. He smiled.

"You were once the Queen of Atlantis. Your son was the King in the final years of the continent. I took over from your son in the final time period."

The bombshell was not one the Queen was expecting. She sat back. She was now totally disarmed. Winston left his stiff-backed chair, and retired to a comfortable chair near the window of the office, in Buckingham Palace. He took off his suit coat, and loosened his tie. The Queen left the protective barrier of her desk, and sat in another comfortable chair across from him. There was tea for them. At some point, they would have sat in these chairs for tea.

"I have had many visions since I left London. My ancient past has become clearer. You were the Queen of Atlantis, one of its greatest rulers. You died of old age. The kingdom of Atlantis had grown fractious. Technological advancement was supreme, but abuses were rampant. The priests had enormous healing abilities, and could access other realms of existence, whether they be space-time scientific dimensions or mystical, spiritual realms, I do not know. Maybe, both. Our society was divided. You had held it together. Your son, the King, could not hold it together. I succeeded him as King in the final time period. The continent fell to the sea during my tenure, but not without enormous effort to save it."

The Queen was still speechless. It all seemed so true. She felt the truth deep inside her.

"I am sure there are many traditions, legends, lore, secrets, magic, customs, knowledge, and history that only the Crown knows. And that this is passed on to each new monarch," Winston gave his cue for the Queen to take the bait, or pass. The Queen smiled broadly, almost in a maternal way, Winston thought.

"I feel everything that you have said. I felt your enormous presence at Windsor Castle. Now I know. Not only a King, as to which I had been advised, but a son in a different, ancient era. Welcome home!" the Queen felt tears streaming down her cheeks. She was flushed pink in her cheeks.

Winston wanted to ask her about any knowledge about Atlantis, or its energy crystals. But he deferred to the modern monarch. He was not a King in the present world, notwithstanding the chants of those he healed. But the Queen took a sip of tea, and then held the cup out with her right hand, her pinky finger in the air. She took his bait, hook, line and sinker.

"We have passed on unsubstantiated tales about Atlantis, and the preservation of its books and records, and yes, the crystals. We do not know the location of that Treasure trove. There was a King in the fourteenth century who allegedly had healing powers. There may be crystals still in London. Or another energy source. But we think the Treasure trove is long gone."

Winston was at his highest attention. He locked in on her every word.

"We think it is in a lost cavern in Africa, the Cavern of Lost Treasures. There is a secret society that stands today. It is similar to the Templar Knights. It exists in the minds of conspiracy theorists, and it exists in the shadows in reality, too. They have been searching for the Treasure trove for centuries. They know not of Atlantis. Only the monarchy has that knowledge. They want to find Excalibur! And proof of the existence of King Arthur and Guinevere, their crowns and jewels. But, Winston, we do not know where the energy sources are, or the crystals. The legend of the crystals does carry on. But it rests with me, and I only know of the legend," the Queen lowered her cup.

Winston suddenly realized that the Queen was hoping he could answer those questions, the same questions that he had.

"I see now that you had hoped I had the answers."

They stared at each other, almost in a stalemate. Winston spoke again.

"I have visions. I may have more. Together we can seek out this Treasure trove, and solve the mysteries of our former continent. And find the English legendary Treasures, as well. My healing powers may not even be from a power source or the crystals. They may be from within, from another realm or dimension. Or possibly the energy source, from the crystals or elsewhere, enables me to enter another dimension where technology is available to heal, like the regenerative technologies that will be available in the future through genetic manipulation and transformative master cells. As an aside, the crystals could benefit the world with wireless, free energy."

The Queen perked up again. She felt enlivened. Her disappointment disappeared as fast as it had arrived. But then she raised her right eyebrow. Winston took the cue. He knelt in front of her, and he grabbed her hands and held them.

"I am the once and former King of Atlantis. Upon my word, you shall be healed. So, it shall be said, so, it shall be done. You are hereby healed. Go, and serve the common good."

The Queen stood at the same time as Winston stood.

"Long Live the King!"

She embraced him for a long moment. Her face was radiant. Her aches and pains were gone. She suffered no major illnesses, other than the normal afflictions of old age, arthritis, mild memory issues, and the like. But now she felt refreshed, young and rejuvenated.

"King of Atlantis, of course!" The Queen laughed.

"Of course!" Winston rejoined with a boisterous laugh.

"I see you have a full head of hair!"

"Benefits of the trade, I suppose. But it grew back, or came back, I should say, at the lightning strike in Greenwich."

Winston abruptly stopped talking.

"You don't suppose," the Queen offered.

"I do suppose. The energy was other worldly. The worker, my family, and I should not have survived. But the lightning augmented my powers, whether from the energy source, or from within, or from some universal Star Wars type force, that I did not mention earlier. I may go there tomorrow, assuming Ms. Hollingsworth has not released her epic Tale! I need to be incognito. But she does not know most of what we speak of today. I did tell her my theories, about internal power, universal force, external force, such as from the crystals. So, that may be enough to start a Treasure hunt. But it would not last long."

The Queen looked a little concerned.

"I have worked closely with Becca. I am not sure she wants to publish her Tale. There is risk the establishment will disregard it as fancy and fable, and suggest she retire to write fantasies, and stories about witches and goblins."

"Or there is a risk of hysteria and jubilation, or a religious fervor. The latter I can assure you there is no basis for, but who knows the imaginative power of the public mind. My life would be forever changed. I would be a servant to my powers, and upon failure, a likely candidate for castigation, or allegations of favoritism and cronyism. I want to help people. But an understanding of these powers, to pass on to posterity, would be a better purpose for me.

And you," Winston said in a serious tone, reflecting deeply on his role in the future. "What do you think of her publishing the Tale.

"Becca is free to pursue her goals and agenda. We will wait for her next step. I think the more likely response is one of suspicion, denial or rejection. A pleasant piece to cheer up our dreary lives, might be the review. Maybe that is better. And the most notable healed person, Chester Jones, had an alternative story, one that the press had already confirmed."

"Yes, rehabilitation from massive effort."

"Thank you, for healing me. I will work with you as best I can to find our Treasure trove. But Winston, were you once Winston Churchill? King Arthur? Another King?"

"I see you have harbored many questions for me over the last two weeks. I think not on the Prime Minister, although I feel like I know him well given my readings on him. I think you would know. You knew him. And he was alive, when I was born."

The Queen stared deeply into his eyes.

"No, you were not him."

"As for King Arthur, I believe I had an unborn son in Atlantis. I think he may have back as King Arthur. I believe the legend of King Arthur is real. Let us find his sword! I do not believe I was another King."

"Let us prepare for the gala event. We invited your three golf friends. They will arrive via private jet. And if you can wait on Greenwich, we have a tee time for the four of you at an Open course in England. We will surprise you with that tonight."

"That is tremendous. Greenwich shall wait."

"And the Princess wants to spend the day with Elizabeth, Anne, and Becca. I will take care of Mary's itinerary. SO, the

party, and then a marvelous British day tomorrow. Cheerio!"

"Cheerio!"

20.

KENSINGTON PALACE stood proud that Saturday
night. It knew royalty from two human eras was to
be present. The staff had prepared the Palace to
look its finest. The Queen was first to arrive. She was with
her secretary, as usual, and her son, the Prince, and his
wife, and her grandsons, young Princes, and their Princess
wives. They would form a greeting line for all the guests.
The party was for family, and for the King of Atlantis, and
his flock of healed persons. Her cousin, Charles of South
Hampton, was front and center in the greeting line, with
Abigail Johnstone.

One by one, the attendees on the list were checked off.
They were thrilled and ecstatic to meet British royalty. They
walked through the greeting line, and then partook in hors
d'oeurves handed out by waitresses with trays. There were
tables, with assigned seating only for the royal family, for
the main course, which was served buffet style.

Becca was one of the last to arrive. She came with
Amanda. They both wore beautiful evening gowns, with
their hair in buns, pearl necklaces, and dazzling earrings.
Both had been silent on the cab ride over. There was a
nervousness, and intensity. They loved each other dearly,
and wanted the best for each other, but they were focused

on Chester Jones. What would he do? Who would he like? Let him decide. To the victor, goes the spoils.

Chester Jones arrived moments later, with James Tudor. Both looked so handsome to Becca, in their fine tuxedos. All of the men were wearing tuxedos or the finest suits. Amanda feigned indifference, and walked to the food station serving farm fresh chicken galantine with chutney and a chicken and broccoli baked pasta. She grabbed some white wine on the way. But then she saw a young man, quite handsome, and very athletic. There was something about him.

Chester was greeted by the three Princes, who marveled at his great skill and scoring abilities. They knew now he had been healed by the King of Atlantis, and not through some marathon rehabilitation program, as the public and his fans still believed. They talked football for what seemed like an eternity for Becca. Winston and his family had not arrived. Becca had invited the attendees individually. She did not tell them that the King would be in attendance, other than a chosen few. But as the party goers met and conversed with each other, they realized, that other than the royal family, all of them had one thing in common. They had been healed by the once and former King of Atlantis. The buzz started to grow louder.

Becca was talking to Chauncey Parsons. He was in his best attire he had ever worn, and looked smashing. He tried his best to woo her attention and affection. She barely heard a word he said. Bart Tower, using the moniker Bartholomew on this night, casually joined the conversation. He threw his two pence into the ring for her affections, as well. She looked resplendent. She even saw one of the young Princes had noticed her. She smiled and curtsied. He merely looked away, caught in his indiscreet ogling. She left when Bart and Chauncey started to talk about football.

On her way to the table, John Masterson stopped her. She shook his hand. He gave her an update on the rapid progress his company was making in its preparation of products for the marketplace, and its continued research and development. She acknowledged him, but turned skillfully away to walk with the passing secretary to the Queen. All of the men chasing her watched her drift away. But they stopped their courting when Chester Jones broke free from the clutches of the Princes, to approach her.

"I think you may have someone to talk to," the secretary said to Becca, turning her head in the direction of Chester Jones. Becca hesitated, and just turned on a dime, with a breathtaking smile and a casual turn of her head.

As she turned, she saw Amanda beaming and flirting openly with a young man she had not seen before, and who was not on the list, at least her list. Maybe he was a cousin of the royal family. She heard his accent. It was from down under. *OH, the surfer dude! He is adorable! I am glad he is here, and talking to Amanda. But who does Chester like?*

And she saw young Mark Buckingham talking to Rose and Shaylee. *It never changes, I suppose. They are so young.* She saw Jess and Joss frolicking with Starr and Sensa. *Four Granddaughters who will be life-long friends.*

Houston Garrison was locked into a deep conversation with Chauncey Parsons. She overheard them talking about a new business venture. The other three kids, two boys and a girl, from Hyde Park were soon joining the fun with Shaylee and her new friends. Mark chummed up with the two boys, and the four girls and they all started to dance, to the music from the small band that started to play. The mothers of the Hyde Park kids were joined in conversation with Aunt Grace and John Masterson's mother. They all played bridge and were scheming the founding of a new group.

Soon some barking could be heard. Jackson ran to the band and back to Johanna and Savannah Stark. Everyone cheered loudly for Jackson. Amanda went to the barking. She held the dog close to her bosom. She wished her dog had been saved. She shed a tear for him. She walked away. Elizabeth grabbed Jackson, and would not let him go for a few minutes. She loved animals so much.

But everyone in unison seemed to pause. Where was the King? As if on command, they shouted in a melodic and re-peating chorus, "Long Live the King! Long Live the King!"

The Queen had walked to the entrance of an adjacent room. She pulled back a makeshift curtain, and there they were. Chester was now standing next to Becca. She grabbed and held his hand. He smiled at her, and gently squeezed her hand. He whispered, "I am sorry for leaving you so long ago! I am a new man! And it is you that I thought of the most all of these years alone and on the street. Amanda was wealthy beyond all means, and I just was attracted to her family and wealth. I am over that now. I am so happy she has been healed, too, by the King. I know now that I snick-ered at her looks along the river, not knowing it was Aman-da. I just apologized to her. She seems entranced. I know the surfer from the museum. But you know, I have always loved you!"

Becca was thrilled, and startled. All she could muster was an "I love you, too!" Then the attendees roared.

"May I introduce to you the two Princesses of Atlantis, Elizabeth and Anne!" the Queen stated regally, extending her arm toward them as they entered the room. The roar was loud.

"And the wife of the King, Mary!"

The roar continued.

"And the man who healed you all, with great power and energy from within, from the energy of our great kingdom in England and greatest city on earth, London. Hail to the King of Atlantis. Long Live the King!"

The crowd burst into the loudest roar ever heard in the Palace. One of the Princesses gazed up at the ceiling to make sure it was not falling. Chants continued. Energy was swirling through the Palace. Auras were illuminating. Suddenly, everyone could see the auras of the others. A powerful surge of love and positive energy engulfed the attendees. Each soon drifted into higher states of consciousness, or alternated realities, or space-time dimensions.

All soon were in the Palace in Atlantis, in their altered states. They gawked at its beauty, and walked to the windows and open porticos to gaze at the pounding surf, of what they suspected was the Atlantic Ocean long ago. Giant water fountains and sculptures of great Atlanteans adorned the Palace floors. Paintings of Atlantean landscapes and former Kings and Queens hung from the walls. Soon, ghost like figures walked through the room They were such taller, maybe ten feet tall, and the men were very broad shouldered, and the woman very curvaceous and robust. Many had red hair, but most were blonde or brown haired. Their eyes were blue like the ocean. Their skin appeared bronze.

They saw what looked to be flying ships outside, powered by an invisible silent source. The countryside to the west was rolling and green, and looked remarkably like the English countryside. Creatures stalked outside. Their forms looked unrecognizable, save for in ancient Egyptian hieroglyphics. Maybe they were centaurs, and other hybrid animal and humans depicted in the Egyptian scripts. The clothes appeared roman like in style, but the fabric looked like it was synthetic with technological advancements. Holograms appeared everywhere. The ghosts carried devices, that seemed to be connected to a wireless power source, and wireless communications source. *Like our smart phones, many of them thought.*

But as they continued to ooh and ah over their vision of the ancient past and kingdom, they saw jet black storm clouds, and violent churning seas. Red lightning lit of the sky. Then other colors of the rainbow illuminated the sky. Thunder boomed, and the ground shook. The King, wearing a luxurious regal cape soon spoke to them.

"Time to go back home."

With a snap of his fingers, the attendees drifted back to their current reality. Those who had not been healed before, like the band members, waitresses, cooks, guards, and other staff had all gone on the magical voyage, and all were healed of their maladies and ailments.

The stunned crowd stayed silent. They awaited a command.

Winston grabbed the Queen's hand and raised it to the air. "Hail to the Queen!"

The attendees chanted back in unison.

"May all of you prosper in peace and happiness. And continue to serve the common good, and make your mark on the world in a positive way," the King said.

No one spoke.

"But have fun tonight, make friends, and social and business contacts, and dine, drink socially, and dance and party on this fantastic and historic evening!"

The attendees roared again. Branden Dunster took the mike and introduced the dancers in order. The Prince danced with his mother the Queen, first. Then Charles and Abigail. Winston and Mary danced a waltz. Yes, they knew how to ball room dance, too. The Prince and his wife, and the young Princes and their Princesses then danced, also, in ballroom style.

The floor cleared. Soon there were just two individuals on the floor. It was Becca and Chester. Everyone was silent. Chester took her hand, and held it high in the air. She accepted his advance, and soon they were ball room dancing to the delight of the attendees.

Branden Dunster then opened up the dancing to all, playing his international hit single, all envisioned in Camden, that fateful day he met the King. The young boys and girls soon jumped in and danced modern style. The whole room soon frolicked. Amanda furiously kept pace with Peter Taylor, her new found paramour. Bart had curried the favor of the girl who had a new hand, replacing the one lost in the boating accident. He had often noticed her walking under London Bridge. He was ecstatic. Bart had also found the other three healed persons on Saturday night. The young lad had befriended the Hyde Park bunch. The mental patient, a man in his fifties, now had fallen in love with the woman following the moonlight, now free of cancer. The man with arthritis just sat back and watched. He was an artist. His mind was filled with ideas for new paintings. Alfred Jackman held his wife were in a deep embrace, as did Pete Copperfield with his wife. The Windsor Castle guard, with his strong new knee, danced with the mother of John Masterson. John Masterson stopped in his tracks. She had been there all night. But he had not seen her. It was his childhood and early adult girlfriend, who he had unceremoniously dumped. She was here. Jenny Smithson. She ran to him, and hurled herself into the air. He caught her and kissed her passionately for the longest moment. Tears of joy flowed down their cheeks. James Tudor then saw his former wife. He thought she was gone forever in the United States. They embraced in deep love, and danced feverishly, like they were known to do. They were expert rug cutters. Chauncey Parsons fell head over heels in love Nurse Wanda. His new best friend, Houston, danced with Nurse Beatrice. They danced their hearts off. The Romeo and Juliet crowd, mostly couples, soon took over the dance floor. They partook and in a perfectly choreographed waltz, reminiscent of the sixteenth century. Some thought it was a harbinger of the return of Queen Elizabeth 1. Thoughts that Elizabeth may be the former adored Queen soon swept the dance floor. Elizabeth was dancing with her sister when the floor opened up.

She waved to them, but said, "She is not I!" The crown moaned, but continued the festivities.

Charles and Abigail were the first to leave, with a gracious applause from all. Grace Bennington, was next to leave. She thanked the King and the Queen. She took Starr and Sensa home, dreaming about the possibilities for her two blessed granddaughters. The caddy, Peter and his two granddaughters, Jess and Joss were next. Peter whispered to Winston that he had earned his professional golfer status back. "Who knows!" he laughed.

Amanda and Peter Taylor departed without a good-bye, just a happy wave, that was returned by the Queen, the King, and all three Princes. The theater crowd left in orderly fashion, all friends for life, and headed back to their travel bus that they had taken together. They were singing, mixed with chants to the King and Queen.

The four mothers and their kids, including Merle Smith and her daughter Shaylee, left together, too, forever bonded. Bart Tower and Rose caught a ride home with Alfred Jackman and his wife. Amanda soon ran back into the ballroom. She grabbed Aunt Grace and Mark Buckingham. Mark had a holster full of contact information for some very pretty young girls. He high fived the King and one of the young Princes, as his wife, the Princess, giggled in amusement.

The two Johns, Tudor and Masterson, soon left with their reunited loves from the past. Mrs. Masterson happily escorted them.

The Princes and the Princesses left smiling broadly. Most everyone departed quickly.

The Queen and her secretary left for one of the state rooms. Chester was disappointed he could not follow. Becca kissed him deeply. The secretary soon returned, and whispered something into Winston's ear. The secretary then left the Palace. Becca spoke to Chester.

"We shall meet tomorrow by the River Thames, on your sacred place!"

"Indeed!" And off he went, gleefully into the night.

Winston said good-bye to his golf friends. They were flabbergasted and exhausted. He told them of their golf round on Sunday. They were thrilled. He had decided not to play, but a new Professional, a certain Peter McAllister, would join them at Royal Birkdale. Winston had just played there, and wanted to be with his family.

Winston kissed Mary goodnight. Elizabeth and Anne, too. The three of them would spend the night in the Palace, much to their delight.

Winston held Becca's hand, like he would one of his daughters. Up the stairs they went to the state room with the Queen.

21.

WINSTON LOOKED over at the Queen. All were tired from the festivities of the evening and its gala party. Becca was exhausted. She bobbed her head, trying to keep her eyes open. She fell into a deep slumber.

Winston spoke first.

"As eventful as the evening was, we have one last stop. One last journey. Come over here next to me."

The Queen sat next to Winston on a couch.

"I do not know where the location of where we are going. I saw it in a vision. I believe with all the energy that is still rampant in this Palace, I can take you there, by way of a vision, or teleportation, or shift in realms, or space-time dimensions, just as we all went to the Palace in Atlantis this evening. So, HOLD ON!"

Winston grabbed her hands, and off they went into a deep slumber.

Soon they saw each other, whether as spirits, or disembodied souls, or transported bodies. They drifted away and soon awoke in a spectacular cavern, filled with iridescent lights. The Queen gasped.

"It is all true. I knew it! The legends are true. The Cavern of Lost Treasures is real."

They traversed the Cavern slowly.

"We don't have much time," Winston noted.

They could hear an internal mountain stream drifting gently down its path. They turned a corner, and a large room lay before them. Hundreds of Treasures, jewels, armaments, and ancient artifacts stood before them. At the end of the room, were large crystals. But the corner of the room drew the attention of the Queen, as if it were calling her. She steadied herself and made her way to the corner.

She knelt down and wept. She closed her eyes and said a prayer to her God, and to her former Kings and Queens.

"Hail Ye King Arthur!" She bowed down. She then raised her hand and reached out and held the greatest sword of all time. She held Excalibur!

After moments of awe, she stood. She was beckoned again. This time she saw the Crown of King Arthur, and the Crown of his Queen, Guinevere. She bowed again.

"Hail to the first King and Queen of England!"

She was mesmerized and astounded, but ultimately, very joyful. She turned to Winston.

"And the great Treasures of Atlantis, too?"

"Yes. Great tombs, treatises, books of wisdom, drawings, artifacts, and some of the crystals. Indeed. Wealth of the ages. And England's most sought after Treasures."

The Queen held her gaze, searching for more confirmation and knowledge.

"I believe this is the Cavern of Lost Treasures, yes, you are right.! But its location, I do not know."

Winston looked at the Queen. He walked over and sat on an iron throne. It may have been from Atlantis. The Queen suspected it may have been the throne of King Arthur. Winston spoke again.

"I gather your ultimate interest in me was the link to this Cavern of Lost Treasures to Atlantis. But your interest has always been the lost English Treasures, mostly Excalibur, and the crowns you see now before you," Winston examined the Queen as he spoke.

"That is true. We thought there was a relationship there that would lead us to the Treasures. But the Atlantean technology and power sources, although seemingly mythical and far reaching, held our interest as well. They could so benefit humankind and our planet."

"I agree. A new journey!"

Winston stood from the iron throne. He held the Queen's hand and walked to the edge of the gentle soothing stream.

"And there is more. I had an unborn son in Atlantis. He perished in the womb of my Queen, when the continent submerged into the ocean. I have had visions that he has returned, and may be in Africa, but maybe in America, I am not sure. I suspect he is still young. He may seek to find this Cavern of Lost Treasures! But, I do not know who or where he is. The visions are not in the real universe that we perceive every day. As I said, I do not know the location of this Cavern, either. But, a good start is Africa, based on the legends passed on to you throughout the generations and ages. And that he may be here corroborates that hypothesis."

The Queen listened intently, her mind racing. She thought back to the events of a decade or so ago. Could it be?"

"You may want to let the Princes know of my unborn son."

"Yes, I shall."

The Queen looked at Winston now as an ally and an equal in royalty. She did not want to hide anything from him.

"And I have one more thing."

"Yes?"

"I may know who your unborn son is."

"Fantastic! And!"

"But we lost him. And we don't know his name or location. I thought he may have perished. I am encouraged he may be alive."

"Another journey!"

"Indeed!"

Silence overtook them, as they surrendered to the depths of thought. Soon they sojourned back to the present time and Kensington Palace.

They awoke just as Becca awoke.

Becca turned and addressed Winston.

"I am not going to report your story in the newspapers. I am not sure many will believe it, particularly, the events of tonight. I am staying with the rehabilitation story for Chester."

"That is fine. But I am fine even if you report it. I would like to remain anonymous, but even that is up to you."

"No, I have gained so much. I owe you so much. And the story is a Treasure that should remain with the Kingdom of England, to be passed on through the ages!"

"Great. I am think it is time to retire for the evening."

Becca looked up again.

"But I am going to author a Tale. A fairy tale, to most! I shall let you read it. I will publish it as fiction. With fictional names."

"I am fine with that, too," Winston said.

"I, too," the Queen agreed.

The title shall be "A Healer's Tale London."

"Fantastic!"

"And I am using pen name."

"OK."

"The name I heard as the King of Atlantis!"

"Indeed."

And they all retired for the evening in the Palace, filled with dreams, fantasies, visions and thoughts of the future.

Postscript

The author's pen name is King Atlas V. King Atlas V was once an Olympic hero in Atlantis. He later became King of Atlantis in its final months to save the continent from destruction. He did not succeed. Atlantis was a highly developed and technologically sophisticated society. In the 2020s and beyond mankind will match that success in technology. Hopefully, mankind will not make the same mistakes as the people of Atlantis did.

ABOUT THE AUTHOR

The author now lives in Florida with his wife of over thirty years. He has keen interests in the future, legends and myths, the dream world, alternate realities, healers and, sports. He writes of the dreams of the fantastic and the mythical, so that others can enjoy those dreams. Check out other books written by the author at: https://www.amazon.com/author/kingatlasv.

www.ingramcontent.com/pod-product-compliance
Lightning Source LLC
Chambersburg PA
CBHW050848180626
46814CB00007B/2683